Mommy in Training
SHELLEY GALLOWAY

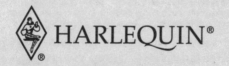

HARLEQUIN®

TORONTO • NEW YORK • LONDON
AMSTERDAM • PARIS • SYDNEY • HAMBURG
STOCKHOLM • ATHENS • TOKYO • MILAN • MADRID
PRAGUE • WARSAW • BUDAPEST • AUCKLAND

Recycling programs
for this product may
not exist in your area.

ISBN-13: 978-0-373-75248-5
ISBN-10: 0-373-75248-2

MOMMY IN TRAINING

Copyright © 2009 by Shelley Sabga.

This edition published by arrangement with Harlequin Books S.A.

® and TM are trademarks of the publisher. Trademarks indicated with ® are registered in the United States Patent and Trademark Office, the Canadian Trade Marks Office and in other countries.

www.eHarlequin.com

Printed in U.S.A.

"What about me? Aren't you worried about disappointing me?"

Minnie glanced at his lips. Wondered what it would feel like to kiss him. Really kiss him.

He grinned.

Suddenly it hit her. Matt knew exactly what he was doing. He knew she had a weak spot for him that had everything to do with a crush that didn't have the decency to go away.

She fought to remain aloof. To remember that his company was about to put her store out of business. "Not particularly. After all, you are my competition."

He stepped back. "Minnie Clark, I can't help it if you don't like my job. Don't be mad at me forever."

Dear Reader,

Thanks for picking up *Mommy in Training!* While some books have seemed to come together pretty quickly, this one sure didn't. Over the past eight years I've written and rewritten Matt and Minnie's story. The only things that stayed the same were Matt and Minnie's characters and my belief that their romance was worth sharing. I couldn't be more pleased with how the story turned out.

I enjoyed writing *Mommy in Training* because it allowed me to think about Texas and remember everything I love about the Lone Star State. I grew up in Houston, and my husband and I spent the first five years of our marriage in a little town north of Dallas. Through Matt and Minnie, I got to go back to places where everyone knows each other, heat and humidity are nothing to take lightly and where a trip to the grocery store means putting on a fresh coat of lipstick.

So, though it's cold outside, I hope you'll take a little break with Matt and Minnie. Sip some tea. Imagine it being as hot as July, and remember that sometimes the best things just take a while to happen. But when they do, they're certainly worth waiting for.

If you get a moment, I hope you'll join me at my Web site, www.shelleygalloway.com, or at the Harlequin American Writers' blog: www.harauthors.blogspot.com.

Happy reading!

Shelley

ABOUT THE AUTHOR

Shelley Galloway loves to get up early, drink too much coffee and write books. These pastimes come in handy during her day-to-day life in southern Ohio. Most days she can be found driving her teenagers to their various activities, writing romances in her basement or trying to find a way to get ahead of her pile of laundry. She's also been known to talk to her miniature dachshund, Suzy, as if she actually has opinions about books.

Shelley is the proud recipient of a *Romantic Times BOOKreviews* Reviewer's Choice Award for her 2006 release, *Simple Gifts*. Shelley attends several conferences every year and loves to meet readers. She also spends a lot of time online. Please visit her at eHarlequin.com or at www.shelleygalloway.com.

Books by Shelley Galloway

HARLEQUIN AMERICAN ROMANCE

To my editor Johanna Raisanen,
who was instrumental in making
Matt and Minnie's story come alive.

And of course to Tom, who one day introduced me
to a man named Matt—and, well, the rest is history.

Chapter One

"Matt, you're back," Mrs. Wyzecki proclaimed, as though it was the biggest surprise of her life.

Matt knew better. After all, the elderly lady had called his cell phone at least eleven times over the past two weeks, just to double-check that he was still heading in her direction.

But there was no sense in reminding her of that. Surely things hadn't changed all that much in the ten years since he'd lived in her house. "You're giving me no credit. Did you really think I wouldn't show up like I said I would?"

Wanda Wyzecki stepped back to allow him entrance. "It wasn't that I didn't think you'd come back...I just wasn't sure you'd be able to."

"Well, I was." Matt carefully closed the door behind him, using the moment to steady himself. The Wyzecki home smelled exactly like he remembered—lemon-fresh Pledge, tart Pine-Sol, and underneath it all, Ivory soap. Mrs. Wyzecki had always been a big fan of crisp, clean scents.

And, for some unknown reason, him.

"You comin' in or are you gonna stand there all day?"

Just so she wouldn't realize how good it felt to be around her—and how guilty he felt about staying away for so long, he sassed her right back. "I knew it wouldn't be long before you started ordering me around."

She took his elbow and led him into the rear of the house, where the overlarge kitchen lay. Its space had nothing to do with gourmet cooking and everything to do with the number of people who could sit at the cereal bar.

Matt noticed that their pace was slower than he recalled, and Mrs. Wyzecki's arm a little frailer than he remembered. He was glad things had worked out with SavNGo and he could return as promised.

"Have a seat, Matt. Would you like some water?" Before he could answer she was on the move again. "Sit down and let me get a glass for you."

After she set the drink in front of him and he took a few sips, Matt supposed it was time to get to the heart of the matter. "So, you really are moving."

Faded blue eyes told him a wealth of things her words did not. "It's true."

"You sure you're ready to pick up and go? Jim died just a year ago."

"It seems longer when everything here reminds me of him. It's time, Matt." Hopping up again to turn on her kettle, she added, "There's too many memories around here."

Memories were why he'd driven all the way from Philadelphia to Crescent View, Texas, in one shot. Some things were worth remembering. "Maybe after you let things settle in for a while longer, you'll want to stay."

She turned to him in surprise. "And not let you move in after I promised you could? I wouldn't do that. That's not who I am, Matthew."

"I could find someplace else to live," he said slowly. "I feel I'm pushing you out."

"I asked to you to move here, not the other way around. You haven't pushed a bit."

"Well, if you change your mind, just let me know. A year isn't all that long."

"You're one to talk. We both know worlds can change in a year's time."

She was right about that. His world had changed during his senior year in high school. In twelve months, he'd lost his father, moved in with the Wyzeckis and had applied and been accepted at a number of colleges far away from the only place he'd ever known.

Linking her fingers around the glass, damp and pearly with condensation, Mrs. Wy added, "I'm really looking forward to a new place. I went and visited one of those retirement communities. For a good price, I can have a condo near a walking trail. They even have a fully staffed dining room. I'll be able to go out to eat whenever I want."

Mrs. Wyzecki might have just said she was going to take up tap dancing, it sounded so strange. "You, not cooking?"

"Things have changed since you left, Matthew. I don't have a need for macaroni casserole anymore."

That had been a favorite dish. "That's a shame."

"As I said, things change." The pointy chin that he knew so well inched upward. "It has been almost ten years, you know."

He did know.

Her expression softened, and for a moment, Matt was sure they were both back in time. Back when he was a teenager with a chip on his shoulder the size of Rhode Island and had just moved into the Wyzeckis' house.

She'd served chicken and dumplings for dinner Matt's first night there. It had taken everything inside him to keep his mouth shut in between mouthfuls, he'd been so afraid he was going to say something stupid— like it had been a really long time since he'd had a home-cooked meal. Not since his mother had died when he'd been in fourth grade.

"Anyway," Mrs. Wyzecki blurted, transporting him back to the present. "I figure between the two of us, we could get this old place cleaned up and emptied out in no time at all. Then, come September, it'll be all yours."

The change of ownership still felt strange. "No hurry."

"Oh, I think there might be a bit of a hurry. You've got things to do. We both know that."

"All I've got to do is open Store 35, and it's right here in Crescent View. This move can take all the time it needs to. I usually have to live out of a suitcase for my job, so it'll be nice to have a home base."

Brightening, she patted his arm. "I guess the timing was meant to be, huh?"

"I guess so."

The timing hadn't been a coincidence. He'd fought long and hard to get Crescent View a supercenter—the town was dying ever since the GM factory had closed. People here needed SavNGo.

But just as important to Matt was the opportunity to come back as *somebody*. Though he'd been a star athlete, he'd also been the kid without any family at graduation. For years before that, he'd been the kid who didn't have a mom to help out at class parties or watch his games.

He'd also been the kid with the tough, demanding father who gave affection according to how well he performed on the football and baseball fields.

Everyone had known that.

So it was going to be nice to walk around Crescent View without a shadow hanging over him. Without a hint of talk about who he was ever going to become. He wanted to be able to hold his head up high. It meant a lot to him. So much it was embarrassing.

Ever observant, Mrs. Wyzecki narrowed her eyes at his tone. "You okay, Matthew?"

Hearing his name from her lips in that know-it-all tone never failed to bring a smile. "I'm fine."

"When you get settled here, I hope you'll breathe some new life into this old place. Put on some new paint. Maybe add a screen porch." She pointed out the back window to her late husband's pride and joy: the in-ground pool. "All the plant life surrounding the pool is overgrown. The sun hardly hits the concrete around it anymore."

"I can trim the trees."

"It needs more than that. Matthew, what this place needs is a family." She looked him over. "You ought to start thinking about that."

Well, that brought him up short. He wasn't in the family-planning way. At all. "Don't get carried away."

"Oh, one day you'll find the right woman," Mrs. Wy said with a smile. "You'll fill up this house with love and laughter again and life will be right as rain. Right now, it's too quiet. When the night drags on, my mind drifts to how things used to be."

He couldn't help smiling. "Kids running every-where?" The Wyzeckis had always taken in foster kids.

"Yep. Kids and dogs and mountains of laundry. Sometimes I was sure that I had more schedules to keep track of than any big-city CEO."

"You did a fine job managing it all."

"You did okay, too, Matthew."

Barely. "I don't know about that."

"I do."

The way she looked at him made Matt almost believe she was right. Almost. To most of the town, he'd had everything—good looks, good grades, athletic ability. Only people who knew him well realized that inside he was a mess. Unsure of other people, eager to please, and more than a little resentful of things he didn't have— like a family.

Sliding off the stool, she said, "Well, I'll go show you to your room and let you get settled."

They walked up the stairs, Matt following Mrs. Wy with two duffels in his hands. Instead of heading for his old bedroom, he followed her into the "special" guest room. He raised a brow. "I'm staying here?"

"You're pretty darn special, Matthew." She motioned to the window. "Plus, this room has a better view than your old one."

Obligingly, Matt looked out the window. Everything appeared to be the same except that the trees were taller and the houses seemed smaller than he remembered.

Mrs. Wyzecki pointed to a cute little white house with black shutters, a covered front porch and a cherry-red front door. "You'll never guess who lives there now." After the slightest pause, she announced the answer, just like she was the new host on *The Price is Right*. "Minnie Clark!"

The name sounded familiar, though he couldn't quite place her. "Who?"

"Minnie is Paige's little sister." Tapping on the window, she said, "Let's see. When you were seniors, Minnie was a freshman."

Paige. They'd been a couple, off and on for a good nine months right before graduation. Paige had been vivacious, pretty in that Barbie doll kind of way, and a cheerleader. He'd truly enjoyed dating her. Well, until he'd found her making out with one of the guys on his football team. That little encounter had managed to ruin two relationships and empty a bottle of tequila in one fell swoop.

Mrs. Wyzecki pointed toward the neatly arranged flower beds that surrounded the house like a bright ribbon. "That Minnie's such a sweetie. She owns a card shop now, you know. It's got a real catchy name, too. Carried Away Cards."

Turning his attention from the neatly trimmed boxwoods, he eyed his favorite woman in the world. "Why are you telling me all this?"

"I don't know. Thought you might enjoy reacquainting yourself with an old friend. Especially since she took in Paige's child just last year."

Matt had heard about Paige from his buddy Lane, one of the few people besides Mrs. Wy he'd kept in touch with. "Paige died in a car accident, right?"

"She did, though neither Minnie nor her parents talk much about it." With a frown, she added, "From what I understand, Paige and her husband met up with a semi on the highway in Arizona. In their wills, they left Minnie full custody of Kimber."

Still gazing at Minnie's house, Wanda murmured, "It was surely the saddest day you ever saw when Minnie came home with that little girl. They both looked like they were barely holding each other up."

"Are they doing okay now?"

"I suppose. Minnie's not one to complain." With a

steady look in Matt's direction, she added softly, "Never was."

Now what was that supposed to mean?

"Do her parents live nearby?"

"Two towns over. Anson and JoAnn help when they can, but sometimes I think Minnie does better without them around. Anson and Jo can't last more than a minute or two without mentioning Paige and dissolving into tears."

"Which would be hard for Kimber."

"Uh-huh. But that's okay. Me and that little thing have become pretty close. I get a kick out of watching Minnie deal with Kimber. Oh, but she's getting a run for her money!"

She padded to the tiny linen closet and pulled out two towels. "After you get settled, come downstairs and we'll make plans."

When he was alone, Matt sat on the crocheted bedspread and took a deep breath. At the moment, it didn't matter that he'd lost most of his Texas accent around the time he'd been doing his best to climb up the corporate ladder at SavNGo Discounters. It didn't matter that most of the time he lived out of a suitcase, spending very little time in one place—his job of facilitating grand openings of stores kept him on the road.

For one brief moment, Matt felt vulnerable and full of hope. Like he did years ago. Just after he'd buried his dad and realized he had nowhere to go. Well, nowhere until Mr. and Mrs. Wyzecki offered their home and asked him to help with the dishes.

Once again, he felt accepted and wanted. And that— well, that felt good.

Picking up his cell phone, he called Jackie, his

personal assistant. "I'm in," he said, not bothering with small talk. "Anything you need from me right away?"

"Grab a pen, Matt," she replied with a husky laugh. "I always need something from you."

Chapter Two

Oh, it was him. *Matt Madigan.* Spiky brown hair. Eyes as blue as the sky. Perfect jaw. Flawless smile. Shoulders broad and solid. Matt Madigan was standing in her card shop.

Minnie Clark pulled the invoices she'd been reading a little closer to her face. One foot tapped in a nervous rhythm, keeping pace with her pounding heart. Funny how some things never changed.

She still was drawn to Matt like a child with a shiny new penny. Memories of ninth grade came flooding back. He used to wear frayed button-downs and old Levi's. Scuffed boots and his hair a little too long.

She'd worn a perpetual, lovesick expression whenever he was within ten feet.

Of course, he'd rarely said a word to her—he'd been a senior and Paige had been his on-again, off-again girlfriend.

Minnie had just been a mousy replica. Oh, but how she'd dreamed things were different.

Now, years later, here he was, standing three feet away and looking at a row of cards right in her very own store.

As Minnie noticed that those worn jeans still fit his

backside real fine, slowly Matt turned. Walked toward her. Down went the invoices. On the counter went a card.

"So, is that everything, Matt?"

Blue eyes blinked. "I'm sorry…do we know each other?"

She held out her hand. "Minnie Clark." He shook it.

"Hi." He smiled. Her eyes focused on those lips. Those cheekbones.

"Now I remember. Mrs. Wy said you owned this shop. It's real nice."

"Thanks." A moment passed. It felt like an eternity.

Filling the gap, Matt gestured to his right. "I, uh, really the like your front windows."

Minnie turned to where he pointed at her Back To School display. "Thanks. Alice and I tried real hard on them." *Oh, for heaven's sakes! Tried real hard?*

"And, Minnie…I was sure sorry to hear about Paige."

Just hearing her sister's name still brought pain. "I appreciate that. She's missed by a lot of people."

"I suspect so." Leaning forward, Matt braced two elbows on the counter. "I heard you're raising her daughter, Kimber."

"I am."

A tiny silence stretched for what seemed like an hour, or maybe just a couple of seconds. No matter what, it felt too long.

Minnie picked up the card and scanned it. "Two fifty-seven, Matt."

He pulled out a five dollar bill. "I guess we'll be seeing each other around town some. I'm buying Mrs. Wyzecki's house. Heard you live right across the street."

"I do." She handed him his change. "I sure am going to miss Wanda living there."

His eyes narrowed.

Minnie realized she'd effectively said she wasn't looking forward to him being there. Great. Yet another super interchange between her and Matt. "We're real close."

"Oh."

She pasted on a smile. "If you need anything…just let me know."

"Thanks. I'll do that."

Minnie watched as he walked to the door. She was tempted to ask exactly why he'd come back, what he'd been doing since he'd been gone. But it wasn't the time and, frankly, none of her business.

As a matter of fact, she should know better than to even care. She had Kimber and work. And, well, it hadn't been all that long since Peter had dumped her like a pile of logs. Only six months.

She did not need to be mooning over Matt Madigan.

At least not anymore.

EVERY ONCE IN A WHILE Kimber would do something that was exactly like Paige. An idiosyncrasy that made Minnie want to laugh and cry all at the same time.

Or, like at that very moment, want to go back to bed and retreat from the world because things were just too hard.

This was one of those moments.

Arms folded across her chest, the five-year-old held her ground. "Why can't I go down the street by myself? I'm real good on my bike."

Minnie's dad had taught Kimber to ride a two-wheeler last week. Now, in the little girl's mind, there was no turning back.

"Kimber, you just learned to ride. You're not ready to go out by yourself."

"I am, too."

"No, I don't think so. You don't even know everyone around here yet. What if you got lost?"

"I won't."

"But you could. Sweetheart, if something happened to you, I'd be so sad. Besides, it's too early to go out and play. It's only seven. Most people are still eating their cereal." Minnie pointed to the little girl's bowl, a pile of soggy rice puffs floating on the top. "Sit down and eat."

"I'm done."

"Then you'll just have to be patient. I'll have time to go out with you in an hour."

"That's not fair."

"Oh, well."

"I wish I was home." With a scowl Kimber went back to her room and closed her door, just as Paige had done when she hadn't gotten her way.

And Paige had *always* wanted her way.

For a split second, Minnie glanced at the phone. She could call Mrs. Wyzecki and ask for advice. In a flash, Wanda would stride over and come to the rescue.

It's what she'd done ever since Kimber arrived. Time and again Minnie wondered why Paige had named her Kimber's guardian. Not her parents.

Had it been because they were closer in age? Or was it because Paige had figured Minnie would never have her own kids?

Or had Paige just not been thinking? Her sister had always been the type of girl who never thought anything bad would happen.

And usually nothing ever had.

From birth, Paige seemed to have been born under a lucky star. School had been easy for her. So had everything else. She'd never had a weight struggle, never had a pimple that she couldn't wish off her face.

Boys had liked her, college entrance exams had, too. Paige had not only gotten into every university she'd applied to, but had been awarded scholarship money, as well.

Yep, Paige had been the type of woman who people stopped and stared at. She'd been striking and confident. Polished and successful. Her husband, Jeremy, had been the same way. They'd gotten married in Jeremy's hometown of Phoenix and began their careers. Two years later, Kimber had been born.

Yes, Paige's life had been perfect. So perfect she'd never had a problem reminding Minnie of that.

Which was yet another reason she and Paige had never been especially close.

Minnie was trying to do her best by Kimber, who was willful and grieving. But most of the time, her best didn't seem good enough. Once more, Minnie imagined everyone around her knew it. Peter sure had.

Chapter Three

Matt tried to remember the last time his arms had felt like they were on fire. In high school when the coach had called practices both morning and night? Last January when he'd hired that personal trainer who'd damn near killed him in one session?

As he gingerly stretched his arms overhead, Matt wished he'd been lifting weights with a little more frequency. Maybe then he wouldn't be glaring at the thirty boxes of hardcover books he'd just sorted, packed and lugged to the garage. They now sat in the middle of two bedrooms' worth of furniture and a box of cast-iron pots and pans.

He was coming to find out that everything in the house was practically built of lead.

"You sure you want to give all of these away, Mrs. Wy?"

"Positive." As if to show him that she had no problems with muscle strain, she gamely tapped her temple. "I've got a whole storage closet worth of memories in here. Besides, the library has a new bestseller program. I can get most any book the month it comes out now, so I don't have to buy the books anymore."

"But these are in good shape."

"Brigit at the library wants them, so they'll be put to good use. They're sending a truck here to pick them up."

"I'm glad of that." At first Matt thought he was going to need to transport the books to the library, too. He wouldn't have minded, but his back and arms were already releasing a heartfelt sigh.

Sitting on one of the stacks of boxes, perched on the edge like a parakeet, so bright and vivid in her yellow and lime-green jogging suit, Mrs. Wy said, "Matt, we've been moving things out here for a whole week. Have you noticed that the place isn't looking much emptier?"

He'd noticed that from the moment he'd lugged down a mattress and discovered five storage containers underneath it, each filled to the brim. "You, Mrs. Wy, are a pack rat."

She laughed. "I didn't think I was…but you may be right."

"You have four different sets of china."

She twisted her lips in a pretend pout. "And darn if I can't use but one cup and plate at a time. Well, don't worry about that. Minnie's going to be here any minute to look at those dishes."

That brought him up short, though he didn't really know why. Minnie Clark had been a nice kid at one time, and seemed nice enough now. She was pretty to look at, if you were more into the girl-next-door type instead of cover-girl wanna-be's.

"You close to her?" he asked, figuring he might as well get her whole story since Wanda seemed to be bringing her name up on a regular basis.

"We have gotten close over the years. Minnie is the type of genuine person that comes few and far between."

Mrs. Wy lowered her voice, even though there was just the two of them in the warm garage. "Her last beau was handsome as all get-out, but a real stick-in-the-mud, I'll tell you that."

Before he knew it, Matt was perched on a box of books, too, looking out her garage opening at two rows of rosebushes and feasting on gossip. "What happened?"

"Peter decided to move on to a bigger city and left Minnie in a state of shock." She lowered her voice. "He'd led everyone to believe he was going to propose."

"He never did?"

She paused and blew out a heartfelt sigh. "Nope. I tell you, when Minnie came knockin' on my door, all teary-eyed and sputtering, I was sure she was going to be flashing a diamond, not telling me a tale about how Peter had cut and run. She was in a sad state, I'll tell you that."

Crossing her knees, Mrs. Wy confided, "I heard his rejection had a lot to do with little Kimber. He didn't want any part in taking care of another guy's child, even though that little dear is just about the cutest thing you ever saw."

Though Matt guessed he could imagine some men not being too interested in a rival's child, holding it against Minnie for taking in her orphaned niece was a whole other matter. "That guy, Peter, sounds like a—" he tried to come up with a term safe for a lady's ears "—jerk."

"Oh, he was a jerk." Folding her arms over her chest, Mrs. Wy nodded. "It's good he went. I never liked him anyway. But he could have been nicer about everything, you know? There was no need to just go on out there and trample poor Minnie's heart. Especially when she was trying to do her best. Nobody deserves that."

Matt was saved from saying a word by a sunny

greeting from the topic of conversation herself. "Hello? Wanda, you around?"

"We're in the garage!"

Footsteps click-clacked on the cement walkway that led from the front of the house to the garage in the back. Before he knew it, Matt was returning a smile just like the one Minnie was gifting Wanda with. "Hey."

Her steps faltered. After nodding in his direction, she wandered over to his companion. "Wanda, you shouldn't be outside in this heat. It's gotta be ninety degrees in here."

"I'm always cold. This feels better than that blasted air-conditioning."

"You can change the thermostat. Raise it higher, you know. Then you won't be so chilled inside."

"I'm fine, dear." Mrs. Wyzecki pointed to the boxes of china. "Matt brought these out, but it's up to you to choose your set. After you do, Matthew can carry them over to your house."

Minnie glanced his way. "You don't need to do that."

"It's no trouble."

Dark brown eyes finally met his, sparking in him a new wave of interest. Minnie was far more than simply pretty, Matt decided. She was…lush.

Mrs. Wy cocked her head, obviously listening for the pitter-patter of tiny feet. "Where's your shadow?"

Matt liked how Minnie smiled at that.

"Kimber's helping Mom make cookies today."

"I was just telling Matt here about what an angel that little pea pod is."

"I don't know if angel is the best descriptor, but she is a good girl." Her voice softening, Minnie added, "I never knew how much I needed hugs at the end of the day until I had her. Now I can't imagine life without Kimber sleeping down the hall."

Looking for something to say, Matt stated the obvious. "I'm glad she's getting settled in."

A shadow formed behind her eyes. "Well, we're working on the settling in. Sometimes I think Kimber's adjusting. Other times, I don't know if she ever will."

"Give it a while more. Time heals. It always does," Mrs. Wy said.

Matt knew those words were true. Too bad Minnie didn't look as if she agreed. She kept flitting her eyes to him, then to Mrs. Wy, then back to him like a firefly that couldn't stay away.

Minnie pointed to the boxes. "Wanda, I was thinking…I don't need any of your dishes."

"You better take a set, I've been planning on it." Mrs. Wy clucked. "You said you could use them."

"Y'all are busy. And you don't need to bother."

Matt flexed his arms and pretended he felt no pain. Pretended he didn't feel a pull toward her. Something about Minnie made him want to go all he-man. Maybe because she looked so surprised that someone would go out of his way to help her? "It's no bother. Believe me, you don't want to carry them around. Those boxes are heavy."

"Oh. Well, then, thank you."

Matt was just thinking that her show of appreciation was definitely lacking when Mrs. Wy got right to the point. "Minnie? You look a little peaked. Is something wrong?"

"Maybe."

"Well, what is it? Honestly, I haven't see you so sad since that Peter took off."

Minnie visibly winced as she turned Matt's way.

"Please don't tell me Wanda's been telling you about Peter."

"Not too much," he said. But he couldn't help looking at Minnie meaningfully. "Not too much" meant Mrs. Wy hadn't yet told him Peter's social security number.

"I bet." Minnie rolled her eyes.

"What is wrong, then?"

As if they were at a coffee shop, Minnie plopped down on yet another box of books. "SavNGo Discounters is coming. They just put up a big sign in the front field of the old Crocker Ranch."

It took about half a moment for Matt to realize two things. One, Minnie didn't like SavNGo, and two, she didn't know he had anything to do with it.

Mrs. Wyzecki sighed in relief. "I know that, dear. Now we won't have to drive to Wichita Falls for toilet paper."

"One of my customers, Zenia, mentioned that when SavNGo comes, she won't have to come to Carried Away anymore. She'll be able to get her cards and gifts cheaper there." Flipping that thick brown ponytail off her left shoulder, Minnie exhaled softly. "And the thing of it is…I'm afraid Zenia's right."

Matt suddenly felt as if Mrs. Wy's hot-as-blazes garage had just sucked all the life out of him. Usually he surrounded himself with folks who couldn't say enough good things about the coming of his store. SavNGo brought jobs and good prices. Healthy competition.

Now, looking at Minnie, he was terribly afraid SavNGo might cut into her business. It was always a possibility.

While Matt fumbled for a comment that wasn't full of false hope, Mrs. Wyzecki jumped to the rescue. "People will still come to your store, honey. And I wouldn't pay any mind to that silly Zenia Hardt. Everyone likes you. And they like all your cute gifts and fancy stationery. Business is going to be just fine."

"What am I going to do if they don't?" Pursing her lips, Minnie added, "I've been talking to other people in my shopping plaza. Brenda Martin, who owns Mystery Books is worried, too. So is Abel Pierce at the hardware. We've been doing the math, and it doesn't look good. If I lose even a fourth of my customer base, I'm going to be in a heap of trouble. And I've got Kimber."

Matt was surprised. Hadn't Paige left Minnie money for the girl? And…why wasn't Mrs. Wy saying a word about how Matt practically *was* SavNGo? At least to the town he was. Things were getting awkward. He'd just opened his mouth to set Minnie straight when Mrs. Wy spoke.

"Don't fret, honey. We'll come up with something. We always do."

"Oh, I know. I'll figure it out." With a look of apology his way, Minnie hopped off the box she'd been perching on. "I'm sorry I even brought it up. I guess I haven't put the office behind me yet today."

"Don't you worry. Matt here can't seem to stop talking on his phone and that silly blueberry."

"BlackBerry," he corrected. "And I've got work colleagues expecting me to take their calls."

Mrs. Wy harrumphed. "Morning, noon and night?"

"Especially then."

"One day you're going to find out that work won't stop for the day unless you do the stopping." Heading to the door leading into the kitchen, Mrs. Wyzecki fanned herself. "I think I'm going to take a little break for a bit. It *is* warm out here."

As the door shut behind the elderly woman, Matt stood up, too. And, he was just about to tell Minnie the God's honest truth—that he worked for SavNGo— when he took a real good look at her.

She turned his way and then stepped a little closer. When she smiled, a dimple appeared. So did a set of pretty white teeth.

His senses came alive. Suddenly, talking about work seemed like a real bad idea.

Minnie smelled like lemons and something like cherries or spring. Her pink T-shirt clung to her breasts in the midday heat, making it near impossible to keep from sneaking a peek at her chest every time he tried to do the right thing and keep his eyes focused above her neck.

Minnie leaned forward an inch. "So…were you about to say something?"

"No." Actually, no words were coming to mind. Not a one.

"You sure?"

"I mean, it can wait."

"Oh. Well, then I think I'd like these dishes," Minnie said, pointing to a box filled with delicate china covered in hand-painted roses. "Wanda used to serve me tea on this set when I was little."

"All right. I'll carry it over for you." Matt wiped his suddenly sweaty hands against his thighs.

"You sure it's no trouble?"

Matt bent down and stifled a grunt as he lifted the china-filled box. "No trouble at all," he muttered as Minnie Clark, once very young and very forgettable, started leading the way to her house.

And he, Matt Madigan—former high school quarterback and current director of store planning for SavNGo Discounters, aka Minnie Clark's nemesis—was following Minnie like she was the next big thing.

Chapter Four

"Just set that box right here, Matt," Minnie said, pointing to the one clear spot on her back kitchen counter.

As he did that, she asked, "Would you like a glass of tea?"

"Thank you."

Quickly Minnie poured some into a mason jar and handed it to him, trying not to notice that their fingers brushed. That he was standing in her kitchen. To give herself something to do, she poured herself some, too. "This tastes good."

A ghost of a smile lit his lips. "It does."

They'd run out of conversation. After darting a glance her way, he wandered down the length of her counter. "What's all this?"

"Samples. I'm thinking of expanding a bit, hoping to hook some more people before SavNGo comes in. I'm looking into selling some local artists' work and also carrying more fancy stationery." Pointing to the cards encased in plastic, she said, "These run a little on the expensive side, but they're real pretty, you know? Some of my older gentlemen customers love to pick up fancy cards for their wives' birthdays and such."

Matt jumped back as if they were on fire. "They're real pretty."

She laughed. "Don't worry if you couldn't care less. Most men don't think about cards until they need one. And that doesn't happen too often."

"It's not that. It's just that I probably ought to tell you something, but I'm not real sure how to do it."

Minnie wondered what he could possibly have to say to her that would worry him. Maybe it had something to do with Mrs. Wyzecki?

When he still seemed tongue-tied, she playfully patted his arm. "My mother always says it's best to get tough things over with. Just tell me."

"It's not easy."

With amusement, Minnie watched Matt sip his tea, examine her silly 1950's era kitchen clock, run a finger along the edge of her white laminate countertop. "Come on. Whatever it is can't be all bad. What is it?"

"I work for SavNGo."

Thank goodness her glass had been out of her hand! "What do you mean?"

"I'm the Director of Store Planning."

He said that title with a bit of importance, like she was gonna be impressed.

She most certainly was not. "A director?"

He nodded. "I travel around the country, helping to open new stores. It's one of the reasons I decided to move back home right now. Store 35 is about to break ground."

"You came out because it fit in with your schedule?"

"And I wanted to help Mrs. Wyzecki."

Remembering their conversation in the garage, Minnie folded her arms over her chest. "Why didn't you tell me this earlier?"

He played dumb. "When? I've barely been here a week."

"There's been loads of opportunities. Like when you were in my card shop. Like when we were in the garage."

To his benefit, Matt did not point out that it would have been pretty darn awkward to bring up his job while she was complaining about her financial future. "Minnie, I don't go around telling everyone my business."

There it was. To her, he was special. To him, she was "everyone." "Well, now I know. Thanks for telling me."

Blue eyes blinked. "You don't have to put your arms over your chest like I've done something wrong."

She glanced at her arms, then glared at him. "Don't tell me where to put my arms, Matt Madigan."

"Then don't say my name like it's your next favorite curse word."

"It just might be." Memories of her whining about SavNGo kept slapping her in the face. "I wish you would have told me before I sat there and complained about you in Wanda's garage."

"Minnie, I'm not your enemy. I just work for SavNGo…I don't own it. If you have any questions, I'll be glad to answer them. I answer questions about SavNGo for a living."

"No questions come to mind, but I'll let you know." As a matter of fact, Minnie didn't know what was in her mind at the moment. All she could deal with was the sudden loss she felt. She'd been so excited to see him again.

Now he was the reason she was going to lose her business. "I'm not mad. I've just got things to do." She pointed to the long line of cards. "As you can see."

"I do see."

"And thank you, Matt, for carrying over the dishes. It was really kind of you," she said, all super sweet and fake.

He stepped forward. "Minnie—"

The front door slammed, followed by the patter of tiny feet in sparkly purple tennis shoes. "Minnie?"

In alarm, Minnie looked at Matt. Kimber had had enough to deal with without witnessing an argument. For one second, she met his eyes and forgot to be angry. *Please don't say anything,* she silently pleaded. *Please just act like we're old friends.*

"I'm in the kitchen." Turning to Matt, Minnie whispered, "Listen, don't—"

And then, to her dismay, in popped Kimber, a bright smile on her face as big as the Royal Gorge. The smile was unexpected. In her experience, Kimber didn't smile for anyone without a whole lot of coaxing.

Why was Matt different?

"Who are you?" Kimber asked.

"Matt."

"Are you Aunt Minnie's boyfriend?"

Minnie was sure she couldn't blush anymore. "No, he isn't. He's just an old—"

"Friend." Matt leaned closer and held out a hand. "You must be Kimber. Glad to meet you."

With wide eyes, Kimber shook his hand.

"Oh my goodness, look at you, Matt," JoAnn Clark said, hauling in a Tupperware container filled with what had to be a hundred cookies. "It's so good to see you. I had forgotten you were back."

"Mrs. Clark, nice to see you again." He squatted down to Kimber's level. "I like those shoes."

"They're purple." Kimber was all girl. As if she was

stepping right out of *Sex and the City,* she pointed a foot so Matt could have better access.

Matt touched the toe. "Cool sparkly lights."

Floppy bangs that begged for a trim shielded her eyes. "Minnie got them for me. Where did you come from?"

Matt stood up. "Pennsylvania, but I'm here now for good. I'm going to be your neighbor. I'm going to live in Mrs. Wyzecki's home."

JoAnn looked like Christmas had come early. "Did you hear that, Minnie?"

"I did."

Matt took a step back. "I suppose I best get a move on. Kimber, Mrs. Clark, it's nice to see you again."

Kimber blocked his way with a sparkly two-step. "Guess what? I'm getting me a guinea pig."

"When?"

Kimber turned to Minnie. "When did you say?"

She'd never wanted a guinea pig. "Soon."

"I'm gonna name him George."

Matt flashed another smile. "Maybe when you get him, you can introduce him to me."

Minnie was pretty sure that would only happen when it snowed in July.

Chapter Five

"Why didn't Matt tell me that he worked for SavNGo the first chance he got?" Minnie griped as she grabbed hold of a dandelion and yanked hard on its stem. "He had any number of chances to tell me the whole reason he was here, but he didn't."

As a tiny gust of warm wind floated around Minnie's front yard, Wanda repositioned the brim of her floppy straw hat. "Maybe it was because he knew you'd react this way?"

"React how?"

Wanda motioned to the limp weed Minnie was clutching in her hand. "Like you'd pay money for his body to be buried in the ground near here."

In reflex, Minnie dropped the dandelion as if it were covered in red ants. "That's unfair. I certainly don't wish Matt was dead."

"Just maimed?"

"No, of course not." Minnie fumed as she pulled up another weed, grasping it in a chokehold the way she was envisioning wringing Matt Madigan's neck. "I just hate being surprised, that's all. And I embarrassed myself, too."

"Embarrassed yourself? When?"

"I don't know. A couple of times."

"What did you say when he brought the dishes over?"

"Too much." Minnie tossed a handful of weeds into her wheelbarrow. "Wanda, I know you love Matt like he was your own, but you have to try and see things from my point of view."

"Oh, I think I can see your side, plain as day. But I can see Matthew's, too." As if weighing her conscience, she slowly said, "Matthew never could abide conflict or confrontations. He doesn't trust easily, Minnie. I don't know if he ever has."

This was news to Minnie. "Because of his dad?"

"Because of a lot of things. Matt is a pleaser on the outside. He does what people expect, says what they want to hear. It's charming. But unfortunately, it makes all those feelings and emotions inside of him get all bottled up. He hasn't been able to count on too much, you know. His mama died when he was nine, and, well, his daddy had never been the type to listen to complaints or secrets."

Minnie picked up her spade. "Can you keep a secret?"

"Of course."

"Years ago, I had such a crush on Matt."

"Oh, honey. I already knew that." Under the brim of her straw hat, Wanda grinned broadly. "*Everyone* knew that."

Well, that was mortifying. Minnie pushed at the ground with her spade to cover up her embarrassment. "Oh."

Wanda chuckled. "Don't worry, Minnie. You weren't the only girl who was sad to see Matt leave town. And I don't think you're the only one who has entertained a thought or two about Matt Madigan over the years."

Watching a bumblebee zip around her geraniums, Minnie added, "Maybe I'm just thinking about what could have been." She looked Wanda's way. "I guess you remember about Matt dating Paige?"

"I do. I remember she failed him, too." She shook her head sorrowfully. "Oh, Paige. What a mess that girl was!"

"Paige was so mean to him."

"She broke his heart." Incredibly, Wanda was probably the only person Minnie could trust to be objective when it came to her older sister. Paige had been born thinking that she knew everything, and the sad part of it was that most people thought she was right. Minnie sometimes felt that she was the only person to see that Paige had a healthy case of impulsiveness and arrogance that got her into trouble.

Minnie looked down the street, thinking of Matt, thinking of Kimber. "It's not just broken dreams I'm anxious about, Wanda. I'm worried about everything. I'm worried about Kimber. I'm worried about SavNGo coming in and taking away my only means to support her."

"You have every right to be troubled, dear. Those are all justified fears."

Minnie brushed off her hands. That was why she liked her neighbor so much. Wanda Wyzecki never tried to shrug off Minnie's concerns or sugarcoat bad news. From the day Minnie had met her, Wanda had always been the kind of woman to call a spade a spade.

"Have I told you lately how glad I am that you live across the street?"

"No." But the lady's lips twitched. "But I love you, too, Minnie. Don't worry so, okay?"

Minnie glanced at the new pile of weeds next to her

knees, their leaves and stems already shriveling up in the hot afternoon sun. "What should I do about Matt?"

"Whatever you think best, I suppose."

"I'm going to have a real hard time looking at him every day if his SavNGo puts me out of business."

"Some might say you would have every right to feel that way."

"But not you?"

"I've been around long enough to know that feeling bitter doesn't help a person sleep at night. Just like I know that work isn't the only thing that matters."

"The only people who say that are the ones whose jobs are going real well."

Wanda stood up. Minnie noticed that her crisp white capris were still, well, crisp and white, and her red T-shirt looked straight out of the dry cleaners. She, on the other hand, had a coat of dirt all over her.

"I best get going," Wanda announced. "Matthew said he'd help me organize Jim's golf things this afternoon." Looking fondly at Matt's truck, Wanda smiled. "I tell you what, though, no matter how you must feel about that man, one thing just can't be denied. He sure is handsome."

Saying Matt was handsome was like saying the sky was blue. Neither did the reality justice.

As Wanda walked back home, Minnie scooped up the last of the weeds and tossed them and her spade into the wheelbarrow. After pulling off her gloves, she walked to her front porch. The shade was a blessed relief. She sat down on one of the wicker rocking chairs and tried to look everywhere besides Matt's shiny black pickup truck across the street.

It was sure hard to realize that heroes were made of flesh and doubts.

"NEVER THOUGHT I'D SEE the day when this field would be made into a parking lot," Lane Henderson said as they watched yet another dump truck roar out onto the street. For the past five hours, earthmovers had cleared out shrubs, grass and rubbish while Bobcats had followed, smoothing over what used to be the Crocker Ranch. "If all goes well, you'll be opening right on schedule, in eight months' time."

In less than a year, Crescent View would be making progress. Providing jobs. Giving people like Lane a good bit of money that was sorely needed in the current economy. "Yep. Everything's moving along like clockwork," Matt said.

"The town council couldn't be more pleased. Some are even talking about moving the Chicken and Bread festival to next March."

The Chicken and Bread festival was the town's biggest event. Years ago, Crescent View's founding fathers had decided to capitalize on the three things their sleepy town had going for it: area poultry farms, wheat fields, and the beautiful countryside covered with bluebonnets and Indian paintbrush, a byproduct of Lady Bird Johnson's efforts to beautify the nation's highways and byways. Consequently, Crescent View hosted thousands of people in the summer, people ready to enjoy the beauty of wildflowers and fried chicken. "Think so?"

"Maybe. Lots of tourists come in for the festival. We'll be pleased as punch to show off our new SavNGo while we're at it."

Matt felt a hearty surge of satisfaction. He could hardly count the number of times he'd sat in his Ford pickup and watched a ground-breaking. Usually he oversaw one or two construction sites and did his best to meet with the town councils and local construction crews at the same time. He'd also become adept at putting the best possible spin on the incoming store.

Here in Crescent View, he hadn't had to do any fast talking at all. He genuinely believed that SavNGo was going to help boost the town's economy, and he'd do everything he possibly could to ensure that the vision became a reality.

What people didn't know was he'd done a lot of fast talking to even get SavNGo in the county at all. Not everyone in the company had thought Crescent View had a future.

Lane rolled back on the heels of his work boots. "Things are going to be a lot different round here soon."

That was no lie, SavNGo might have a bad rap for taking out small businesses, but it had also given back to a lot of communities. Jobs were created, other businesses flocked to the areas surrounding the supercenters, and people enjoyed paying less money for everyday necessities. He liked working for the chain.

Of course, he'd never had to come face-to-face with brown eyes that filled with tears at the thought of SavNGo's impending arrival.

"We're real pleased you asked our company to install all the heating and air-conditioning," Lane said. "Henderson HVAC is going to make sure everything goes as smooth as silk."

"I'm sure it will be that way. And don't act like I did you a favor, y'all turned in the best bid. The decision was strictly based on business."

"We're going to do a good job. Crescent View needs this store in a bad way. We need the work now, and we need the jobs it will bring in the future. Did you know a couple of restaurant chains are now considering coming here?"

"I heard."

"Things are going to turn out real good, I just know it. For years I've been putting everything I've earned back into my business. But now things might get a little easier. I might finally be able to put something in the bank." Gazing off toward the twin water towers that marked the entrance of their town, population 5500, Lane grinned. "Shoot, I might have to start thinking seriously about getting married."

"Married? I didn't know you were seeing anyone special."

"I'm not, but it's about that time."

"Remember when jobs and marriage seemed a life-time away?"

"It used to be. 'Course, we had other things on our minds." Looking into the distance, Lane said, "I was going to become a chemist or something."

"You always were damn smart. All I ever wanted to do was move on."

"You did that."

"Yeah. And now I'm back."

"So…how is being here? As hard as it used to be?"

"In some ways, yes." Matt knew his buddy hadn't asked the question lightly. Lane had witnessed his father yelling at him when he'd fumbled the ball and lost the championship game his freshman year. He'd also sat by Matt's side during his father's memorial service. Lane was one of the few people who knew that Matt was haunted by his past.

Changing the topic, Lane said, "My folks asked if you'd like to come over for dinner soon."

"Thanks, I'd like that."

"I'll let them know. How's the move coming along?"

"About as well as can be expected. Mrs. Wyzecki has too much stuff, but we're getting there."

Lane laughed. "She's always had too much stuff. Some things never change. When are you going to officially move in?"

"I'm in enough. And there's no hurry. Wanda's new condo won't be ready for another month and a half, sometime around the beginning of September."

"I don't know how you're doing it, living with her again."

"She and I get along great, and it's not like there's that much involved. She does her thing, and I do mine."

"No curfew?" Lane asked with a grin.

Matt played along. "Nope, she's been coming in before eleven, so I thought I wouldn't press her."

"You know what? I wouldn't put it past her to stay out later than you!"

"Me, neither. That woman's phone rings more than any teenager's."

After another hour, Lane went on his way and Matt stood alone, watching the trucks come and go and thinking for the first time that maybe Lane had gotten it all wrong. All this time, he'd been thinking how good it was to be in Crescent View because it felt familiar and like the only real home he'd known.

But as he thought of Wanda's upcoming move to the retirement condo, the changes that SavNGo would bring, as well as his move back to Crescent View, maybe the opposite was true. Maybe nothing stayed the same. Maybe nothing ever did.

And if that was the case, Matt wondered what he was going to end up holding on to when he finally decided to trust someone besides Wanda Wyzecki.

Chapter Six

Sunday dawned bright and beautiful with yet another argument. Minnie was beginning to think that the sun wouldn't come out without a whole lot of fussing from a certain curly-haired five-year-old. "You've got to come out of the bathroom sooner or later," Minnie called out from her side of the door. "There's no food in there."

"I don't care. I don't wanna go to church."

They'd already gone through this. Several times. "You don't have a choice. It's what we do on Sundays. Besides, last week you said you had fun."

"I don't remember sayin' that."

"I do. Come on, I bet some of those girls can't wait to say hi."

A pause lasted just long enough for Minnie to think she had won. Then all reason went out the window. "George should be able to go, too. I don't want to leave him here."

"Guinea pigs can't go to Sunday school. You know that."

"Then I'm gonna stay here, too. I want to be with George."

Minnie tried the door handle one more time. Shoot, it was still locked. And because she was tired and frazzled and sick to death of trying to do her best, even when she didn't know what that was, she snapped. "Kimber, if you don't start listening, George is going to have to leave us and go to another home. The home of a little girl who minds."

"Nooo!"

The scream and the wails that followed on its heels made Minnie feel like the Wicked Witch of the West.

And, the worst of all things, a liar. Minnie didn't think she'd ever be able to actually give away that silly little guinea pig. George was pudgy and cute and almost cuddly.

Minnie supposed this was what she got for giving in to Kimber's constant request for a pet. In a moment of true weakness, she'd bought the fifteen-dollar guinea pig and forty dollars' worth of guinea pig supplies.

Kimber loved him, and that made Minnie happy. But after finally receiving what she wanted, Kimber had moved on to the next item on her willful agenda.

"Kimber, you're going to have to learn to leave George home sometimes. He needs his sleep and you need to be with your friends. Don't you think?"

"I don't have any friends at church."

No, she didn't. And that's why she needed to keep going to Sunday school. The teacher had confided that after a rough beginning, things were finally on an upward swing. Minnie was about to deliver yet another ultimatum when Kimber shouted, "There's Matt! Hi, Matt!" Minnie heard a creak and a groan as the bathroom window slowly slid upward. "Hi, Matt! You coming over?"

His voice echoed through the crack below the door. "Maybe."

"Please come over. Now. Minnie's being so mean."

"I find that hard to believe. Your Aunt Minnie's about the sweetest person I know."

"Not today she's not."

Minnie heard Matt's boots on the front porch. Great. Just who she needed to see…the other person in her life who was attempting to drive her crazy.

After knocking a few times, Matt turned the knob and peeked in. "Minnie, how you doing?"

She leaned against the wall. "About how you might expect."

"She wearing you out?" Minnie felt his eyes roam over her for a second before meeting her gaze. "Can I help?"

Her insides warred. She wanted some reinforcement, but she didn't want Matt…did she? When Kimber kicked something in the bathroom, the offer of assistance won out. "Maybe. We're in the midst of yet another battle. I seem to be losing." Again.

His lips twitched, telling Minnie that her Kimber problems were not a surprise. "What's this one about?"

"Sunday school, her lack of friends and one pudgy orange guinea pig." A little more loudly, Minnie said, "Kimber, you're about to be in a heap of trouble, and once more, Matt's going to see you be in it."

"You're in trouble, too. I don't like you, Aunt Minnie."

Words from a fuming five-year-old weren't supposed to hurt so much, but they did. Minnie closed her eyes to keep from reacting in front of Matt.

But obviously she wasn't doing a very good job. "Hey," he murmured, stepping a little closer. Close enough for Minnie to smell his aftershave and see the faint shadow of his beard. With the edge of a callused thumb, he gently brushed a wayward tear from her cheek. "It's going to be okay."

Even though she didn't like him— Correction. Even though she didn't *want* to like him, Minnie accepted his touch. "I know. I'm just tired of constantly battling."

"One day, Kimber will be tired of it, too."

"Promise?"

"I've been where she is, more or less. I promise." After treating Minnie to one more reassuring smile, Matt stepped over to the door, rapped a knuckle against the wood and deepened his voice. "Kimber, I heard every mean word you've been saying, and I have to tell you, I'm kind of shocked. Little ladies don't speak to their elders that way."

After a pause, Kimber answered. "They don't?" Her voice was small and insecure.

"No, they don't. Nice girls remember how to listen and say yes, ma'am. Especially with people who love them."

"But Minnie's going to take George away."

"George?"

"The guinea pig," Minnie provided.

Matt's blue eyes danced for a moment before he knocked on the door again. "Open up this door. If you still have that window open, I bet George is about to have heat stroke."

One minute later, the lock clicked and the knob turned. Out peered a very flushed and freckled face. "I'm going to come out now."

Matt crossed his arms. "It's about time."

Face all splotchy, Kimber stepped out, holding a cage tightly. "Minnie, are ya really going to send George away?"

"I should."

Kimber pulled on Matt's cuff. "Tell her no."

"Why do you think I should say that?"

"Because Minnie likes you."

Minnie felt her cheeks heat. "Don't bring Matt into this."

Kimber puffed up her chest like a medieval warrior. "But Matt, don't you see—"

Matt looked tempted. But then he shook his head. "You're making us late."

"Are you going to church, too?"

"I am."

"Really? Why?"

"Learn to be agreeable, Kimber." Minnie felt her control on the situation slipping, which was actually pretty laughable, because she really didn't have any control at all. She didn't know what she was doing with Kimber. She didn't know how to act around Matt Madigan.

Before Kimber and Matt had come back into her life, she'd thought she'd had everything she could handle with Carried Away.

Which just went to show what happened when you started thinking that everything was going to be just fine. Trouble came along. In spades.

Kimber was back to fighting about church. "I don't wanna go. I never get to do what I wanna do."

Minnie stifled a moan. Did that statement come from sheer willfulness and disappointment at their current argument, or was she speaking of other things? Like the fact that she'd been moved across the country and was still having to adjust to new people, new faces and new rules?

Kimber wasn't spoiled, but she definitely had a stubborn streak, not unlike Paige's. Added to the mix was the fact that she was still grieving. It sometimes made the simplest of decisions major battles.

And because the counselors had said that the best

thing for dealing with losses like that was a firm, steady hand, Minnie did her best to be that way. "Kimber, we're not going through this again. Say goodbye to Matt and go put George down."

"But—"

"Or I'm going to pick up the phone and start calling everyone I know who might want him."

After glaring at Minnie, Kimber looked sorrowfully Matt's way. "Bye, Matt."

"Bye, Kimber." As the little girl marched to her room, Matt glanced at Minnie. Now that they were alone, she once again felt the tension that seemed to sizzle between them, just under the surface. "You going to be all right?"

"I'll be fine. Thanks for your help."

"No problem, Min. No problem at all."

MATT HAD JUST SETTLED into the back pew and picked up a hymnal when his cell phone started vibrating. Quickly he fished it out of his pocket and noticed that it was Ben Lambright, the vice president of finance at SavNGo. This call had to be taken.

With a couple of nods in the direction of the folks around him, none looking too pleased that he was getting up and leaving before the service had even started, he moved to the entryway and answered. "Madigan."

"Hi, Matt. Sorry to bother you on a Sunday. I hope I didn't catch you at a bad time?"

With another nod toward the people entering, Matt pushed open the wide oak doors and trotted out to the parking lot, the bright sun blinding him as he did. "Not at all, Ben." After all, if a guy at his level in the company was working on a Sunday morning, Matt couldn't very well say he didn't want to work either. Could he? "How may I help you?"

"I've got some bad news. Second-quarter earnings are about to be announced. They're not good, Matt." He paused. "I've been told to tell you that we're going to need to rebid all the subcontractors for Store 35."

Matt had been through this before. Although the chain was huge, the board and financial officers watched every transaction like a hawk. Two years ago in Arkansas, they'd had to rebid, too. But in Arkansas, he hadn't known a lot of the subcontractors. Asking people to rebid had just been business. This felt vastly different. "All of them?"

Papers shuffled in the background. "All the contracts that haven't begun. You know the drill, Matt. Explain the situation and tell them they're going to have to rebid."

"But—"

"They'll do it, they always do. Cement poured yet?"

"It's scheduled for end of next week."

"Keep the cement contractors, but tell everyone else that we need lower bids, pronto."

"Yes. All right." Matt's shoulders slumped. He'd fought like hell to get Store 35 built in Crescent View.

"It's going to be busy. I appreciate your extra time on this, Matt. You've got quite a reputation of sticking to budget and getting things done the way we want them. I know you'll meet our expectations for Store 35, as well."

"Yes, sir. I'll get back to you tomorrow."

"I'll look forward to it." After a few words about baseball, they hung up. Matt slumped against his truck, deflated.

Nearby, a car zipped into the parking lot and a couple hurriedly unbuckled and then ran into the building, just as the faint hum of the organ and church choir started drifting his way. Folding his arms across his chest, Matt figured his spot outside felt somewhat typical. Once again, he was standing on the outside, looking in.

He'd brought the supercenter to town as a way of trying to do good. Of trying to show everyone that he was worth something. He'd contracted friends of his and local businesses, in an effort to spark the local economy and fire up hope in everyone.

Now he would have to tell Lane that he was going to have to rebid, and most likely wouldn't have near the money he'd planned to have in the bank. His journey into the community's good graces was about to get bumpy.

In fact, the only saving grace seemed to be Kimber, who came over to visit Wanda a lot, and therefore him. Little Kimber who liked him but was so fragile, her moods were mercurial and ever changing.

Kind of like his, come to think of it. More often than not, Matt found himself rethinking every decision these days. He wanted to do the right thing for SavNGo. He wanted to do the right thing for Wanda.

But he also wanted to show everybody that he was just as successful and worthy as they thought he was. Even though inside he didn't feel worthy at all…just a fake.

And then there was the whole Minnie thing. He found her attractive. He found himself thinking about her at odd times, in the middle of the night. Or in the morning, when he had a cup of coffee outside by Wanda's pool.

He wondered about his attraction to Paige's little sister. Was it because she reminded him of Paige?

Or because she was a link to the past?

Or because he felt bad that the store he'd pushed into Crescent View was going to put her business in jeopardy?

Or was it none of those things? Was he merely attracted to her because she touched something in him that made him feel valued and good inside, and worth more than his dad had ever guessed? He wanted her to need him. He wanted to be her protector.

Minnie Clark, the darling of the neighborhood, her family and the town, still seemed so alone.

Was he the only one who thought that was strange?

Chapter Seven

It was Back to School Night. A whole week had passed since the first day of school. And, like the Texas summers that hung with tenacity through August, Minnie felt as though her efforts to get a handle on things were never ending.

With a frown, she tossed yet another sweater set and skirt on the bed and looked down at it. She needed to figure out why she was so nervous and change her attitude, fast. It wouldn't do for Kimber to get a whiff of her vibe. She'd be sure to catch it and adopt a bad case of the shakes, too. Just like the flu.

She knew what was wrong. Plain and simple, Minnie was nervous about being a parent and doing parent things. Hmm. Funny how knowing what the matter was didn't help things in the slightest.

Kimber rolled in with a stuffed bear. "Whatcha doin'?" she asked, hopping up on the rumpled bedspread.

"Trying to get ready to meet Mrs. Strickland."

"She's nice."

Forcing a smile, Minnie said, "I'm anxious to meet her. She's going to tell me all about what you've been doing at school. I want to hear about your progress."

Kimber looked away before speaking. "I wrote my name and made a book."

"Yes, I know. You told me about it. I can't wait to read it."

With a purse of her lips, Kimber nodded. "Mrs. Strickland told me it was okay."

There was something going on that she wasn't hearing. With some worry, Minnie wondered if maybe she was going to get a big surprise. Then, just as quickly, she put all those worries from her mind. It was kindergarten, not high school. Mrs. Strickland was probably going to tell Minnie how Kimber needed to learn to tie her shoes!

"What color sweater do you think I should wear?"

"Blue."

She picked up the set. "Okay. Any special reason you like this one the best?"

"Matt has blue eyes. Daddy did, too."

"Even though you have your mom's pretty brown eyes, I'll wear blue."

They heard a knock on the front door, and Minnie glanced at her digital bedroom clock. "I bet that's Grandpa. He's coming over to watch you."

"Is Matt coming over, too? He still hasn't played with George."

"I don't think so."

Kimber's chin tilted up. "How come he never comes over? I only see him when you let me visit with Mrs. Wy."

"I'm sure Matt's been busy. He's got a real important job." And he hadn't been invited, Minnie privately added. She did not want to see him. No matter how hard she'd tried to fight it, the plain and simple truth was that she still had a crush on Matt Madigan, and he still made her feel all nervous and silly inside.

And resentful.

"I wish he would come over."

"Well, we don't always get what we wish for." Before Kimber could spout off about that, Minnie pointed to the hall. "Go open the door, would you? Grandpa's going to think we're not home."

Kimber went. Within seconds, her father's roaring voice flew down the hall. "You're going to be late if you don't get a move on, Minerva."

"I'm working on it."

Quickly she slipped on the blue sweater set—for Kimber, not Matt—and grabbed her purse.

Minutes later, she gave her dad a hug. "Thanks for coming over. I really appreciate it."

He patted Kimber on the head. "No trouble being with my best girl."

Kimber puffed out her chest. "That's me."

Minnie and her dad shared a bittersweet smile. "Best girl" had been Paige's pet name. "I know it is, honey."

The frantic squeaking of George spurred Kimber into action. "George needs me!"

When they were alone, her dad clapped his hands. "Any directions?"

Her dad could take care of a roomful of kids with his eyes closed. He'd been a great father, and he always seemed to do everything with just enough humor that even the hardest task never seemed insurmountable.

"No, no directions. You know what to do, Dad."

"It's been a while. How about a refresher?"

"All right. Let's see. Bedtime is at eight. Kimber will try to talk her way out of it, but don't give in. Five minutes never works with her, it always morphs into twenty then thirty then a meltdown. Be sure and watch

George. He's chubby but fast. And wily. He can move faster than you'd ever believe."

"Watch the pig. Got it."

"Hmm. Oh. For bedtime, Kimber likes to read *Corduroy,* and she likes to say prayers."

Which brought up something she should have realized her dad would need to be warned about. "She likes to pray for Paige and Jeremy. Then she likes to hear stories about Paige. Sometimes that, uh, takes a while."

Eyes sobering, he whispered, "You've been doing this every night?"

Minnie hoped her shaky bottom lip wouldn't betray her. "Yeah."

Giving her a hug, he said, "You're a pretty good mom, Minnie."

That stopped her in her tracks. "You think?"

"I do. Didn't you hear yourself? You know everything that little girl needs, and you're getting it done."

"Thanks."

He raised an eyebrow. "Of course, you won't get much done if you're late."

And with that, she ran out the door. It wouldn't do to be late for school.

"So you see, Ms. Clark, Kimber's a child in crisis," Mrs. Strickland said.

Minnie's hands shook as she once again fingered her niece's book. She'd written one, all right. Wrote a book all about how everyone she loved was dead and in heaven. It had broken her heart, until she saw the pictures of Matt.

Kimber really liked Matt Madigan.

Aunt Minnie hadn't been mentioned at all.

Minnie felt defensive even though she knew Mrs. Strickland had good intentions. "Kimber went to a counselor for a while. When she said Kimber just needed time, I assumed we were okay."

"Well, I don't know if that's the case. She's behind in everything. She doesn't know her alphabet, and she can't count past ten. She has a hard time sharing and isn't making friends easily. I'm so glad you had time to visit us tonight."

Minnie narrowed her eyes. *Glad she had time?* If Minnie had known that all this was happening—and she hadn't—she would have been a lot more involved.

A lot more.

Actually from the moment she'd arrived at the open house, she'd felt out of the loop. While other parents seemed to know each other, she felt conspicuously left out. When she heard about soccer teams and Brownies, Minnie realized that she hadn't done a real good job of getting Kimber involved socially.

Though she was just a little girl.

Then when she was asked to stay after and talk, Minnie's heart had fallen, feeling once again she wasn't quite doing everything right.

The conversation they were having wasn't helping much, either. "As you know, Kimber hasn't been living with me very long. Just a little over seven months. She's been through a lot."

"And I can appreciate that. However, I have to tell you that no matter what her circumstances are, it's my responsibility to ensure that she learns everything she needs to. Already I'm having serious concerns about whether or not she's ready for our rigorous pace." She paused. "Maybe, Ms. Clark, you'd like to think about putting her in a pre-K program and having her in kindergarten next year?"

"There's only been a week of school. Kimber's a bright girl."

"That may be so, but she's really struggling."

"I can't pull her out of this classroom. It would be devastating."

"So would keeping her in a place where she's unable to keep up. It's not fair to make her struggle, do you think?"

Minnie didn't know what to think. "How about I'll talk to Kimber about her schoolwork and study her alphabet and counting some more? Then we can plan to talk again in two or three weeks."

Mrs. Strickland closed Kimber's work folder with a snap. "Well, you are the guardian. I'll let you make the decisions now…if that's what you want."

Guardian. Not parent. "It is."

Slowly Minnie exited the school, feeling every burden of the world on her shoulders. Her business was about to suffer some serious financial problems, she still felt an overwhelming, fierce ache whenever she thought about the loss of Paige. And now, here was new evidence that she wasn't doing all that well with Kimber, either.

"You okay, Minnie?"

"I'm sorry?" The gal who spoke only looked vaguely familiar.

"Tracy Velasquez." She held out a hand graced with an assortment of silver rings and bangles. "My Nanci is in Mrs. Strickland's class, too."

"I'm sorry," Minnie wasn't sure why she'd been approached. Had Kimber done something to Nanci? Or was she about to get a talking-to about her lack of involvement? "I know we've met before, but my mind was on something else."

"I have a pretty good idea what. Did the iron lady get to you?"

The blunt language surprised a smile. "The iron lady? Is that what you call Mrs. Strickland?"

"Among other things." With a knowing look, Tracy added, "Nanci is my third child. We've been through kindergarten before."

"I'm completely overwhelmed. I didn't know Kimber was supposed to be doing so much."

"Kindergarten is a whole lot more rigorous now than it used to be, that's a fact."

Since she had nothing to lose, Minnie admitted, "There's a chance I may have to pull Kimber and put her in another room. I think that's going to be really tough."

"Want some advice?"

"I want anything you can give me."

Tracy grinned. "Oh, she did give you a hard time! Okay, here goes. First, Mrs. Strickland is an iron lady on the outside, but inside, she's a marshmallow. So, if you disagree with her, don't be afraid to speak up."

"Okay." Minnie felt a little better for insisting Kimber stay in the class.

"Next, she's chewed on just about everyone I know in the ten years she's been at the school. So don't take her criticism personally."

Minnie thought that might be harder to adhere to but agreed gamely.

"Finally, here's the most important thing to remember. Mrs. Strickland really does love these kids. So all her words and such are meant in a good way."

Minnie had a difficult time swallowing that. The

teacher's stern look and veiled—okay, maybe not so veiled—insinuation that she was doing the wrong thing for Kimber stung.

It had been as if Mrs. Strickland had known just where Minnie felt weakest and had gone in for the kill. "Anything else?"

Tracy shrugged. "Maybe…don't worry so much?"

Minnie felt that worrying was her middle name. "That, I don't know if I can do. But, hey, thanks for stopping and giving me these tips. You helped a lot."

"You're welcome. I know with your shop you can't volunteer every week, but try to sign up for a party or something. You'll like seeing the other kids, and you'll meet a few moms. We've all made a vow to help each other as much as possible."

Having a support system like that sounded terrific. "I'll do that."

Chapter Eight

Matt knew what he had to do. It made perfect financial sense, but he hated like hell that it was happening. After directing Lane to have a seat, he perched on the chair across from him. "Thanks for meeting with me."

"No problem, but you could have just stopped by the house or come by the shop."

"I'm afraid this is about business."

"So? We've been talking business every time we've seen each other." Lane chuckled. "What's going on, Matt? You look a little tense. Are you worried Henderson HVAC won't do a good job?"

"No, I read through your references and even went and checked out some of your work. It is good."

His smile faltered. "You checked up on me?"

"I had to. SavNGo has high standards."

All trace of a smile left Lane's expression. "Maybe we should go ahead and get right to business."

"See, it's like this—I heard from corporate. Our second-quarter earnings are down and the stockholders are nervous." Matt opened one of the folders he'd prepared early that morning. "I've been told to cut my budget. We're asking all subcontractors to rebid."

"What? You're saying I'm too high? Now?"

"I'm saying I have to get a lower bid."

"I gave you a fair offer."

Matt looked away, hating that he had to put the company's interests in front of his personal feelings. With effort, he reminded himself that they were talking business. It didn't matter that he'd had dinner at the Hendersons' house just a few evenings ago. "If that bid is the best you can do, I understand. But I'll have to let other HVAC companies bid, too."

Lane slapped his hand on the desk. "You know I'm counting on this account."

"I realize that. And if you do a good job, I'll be happy to recommend y'all's work for future stores in the area. But right now, it's too high."

"That's what labor costs."

"Not for SavNGo. We're used to getting a special rate. I'm going to need you to lower your bid by at least five percent."

"Five percent across the board's going to affect a lot of people." A muscle danced in Lane's jaw. "A lot of people right here in Crescent View. Plumbers, lighting outfits…shoot, even painters and landscapers."

Matt struggled to keep his expression neutral. Lane didn't need to know how hard this was for him. "I realize that."

Lane grabbed the document Matt slid his way and scanned it, running through figures on a calculator he'd pulled from his pocket as he flipped it from page to page. "Five percent is going to mean laying off men who need the work. I've already hired two new guys. They'll have to be the first to go. What am I going to tell them?"

Matt looked at his steepled hands. "Whatever you think best, I guess."

"I thought we were friends. This…this isn't right."

"I have no choice. A VP called me personally, Lane."

"So if he calls, you jump?"

"It's not that. It's the nature of things."

"But this is your hometown."

"That doesn't matter. Store 35 can't be any different than the others. I'm doing what I was told to do, get the costs back in line. It's nothing personal. I hope when you cool down you'll realize that."

Stuffing the calculator back in his pocket, Lane shook his head. "You know, when we heard you were bringing SavNGo to town, people were calling you a hero. But they sure got that wrong, huh?"

"I didn't come here to be a hero." But privately Matt knew he had. Though, just like back when he'd been quarterback, he was learning he couldn't take all the glory or all the blame for what occurred.

Lane stood up. "Can I have a few days to turn in a new bid?"

"I can give you four days, but no more. I'm meeting with other contractors the rest of today, and have a conference call later in the week. I'll need your new bid before then."

"Do you hear yourself? You never mention *names,* Matt. Hell, you don't even mention this *place.* Our town. Crescent View. It's always Store 35."

"Don't be ridiculous. This is hard enough for me without the guilt trip."

"I thought I knew you. I thought you cared about us."

"I do care. How else did you think you even got the store here?" Before he knew it, Matt was spewing secrets he'd hoped to never divulge. "The planners wanted it over in the next county. I'm the one who got the store to *Crescent View*. Things just don't happen."

"No they don't, do they? People make decisions and we all have to live with them. For better or worse."

As the burst of cool air fanned his face, Matt stared at the blank walls of the trailer when he was alone again. He had another five conversations like that to look forward to.

And afterward, Matt knew he would be one of the most resented men in the town.

"I DO LOVE THIS STORE, Minnie," Cora Jean Hardt said as she passed her a twenty-dollar bill. "You have the most unique gift ideas."

"Thank you," Minnie replied, genuinely pleased. Cora Jean was one of her more demanding customers and she'd never been one to dish out false compliments. "I go to Dallas to the gift mart on a regular basis. I've also been trying to stock a good selection of crafts from local artists. I'm glad you like everything."

"You know I do, I'm practically in here every week," she said with a meaningful glance. Cora Jean expected compliments and gratitude.

Luckily Minnie had never minded dishing out heaps of either. "I appreciate your business."

"What are you going to do when SavNGo arrives?"

There it was again, that name reaching across and jabbing her hard and quick, just like a knife into her heart. "I hadn't really thought about it," she lied.

"You should. My sister-in-law Zenia and I were just talking about you the other day, saying how hard it's going to be to buy wrapping paper here when we could just cross over the highway to SavNGo."

"Wrapping paper?"

"People don't want to spend big bucks on things like that anymore." Cora opened up her pocketbook and pulled out a tube of rose-colored lipstick. After carefully applying a fresh coat, she added, "I'd hate to think the wonders of cheap paper would draw customers away from you, but you never know."

Minnie had a whole wall filled with beautiful wrappings, ribbons and bows. She looked at them and saw a one-way ticket to bankruptcy. "You never know," Minnie echoed.

"Yes, things are sure going to get shaken up here when that big store comes to town."

"I think you're right." Minnie thought of Brenda Martin and Abel Pierce again. They'd had yet another meeting to discuss their business futures, but all they'd ended up doing was complaining about supercenters. What were all of them going to do when SavNGo came?

"Yes, SavNGo is the biggest thing to hit Crescent View in quite a while." With a saucy wink Cora Jean added, "Well, SavNGo and Matt Madigan."

Minnie wasn't going to touch that one. After handing Mrs. Hardt the change, Minnie carefully wrapped the ceramic piggy bank in some tissue paper. "I hope your niece likes the gift."

"I know she will," she replied as she breezed away, the door chimes ringing merrily behind her.

Luckily, it was the first time all day Minnie had been alone. The day had been a good one. Real good. After scanning the computer records to review the day's sales, she couldn't help but smile. Business was up from last year. Up by ten or twelve percent. Cora Jean was just getting her riled up, no doubt. Things were going to be fine.

The front door chimed again, bringing in a slew of teenagers…and Matt Madigan, speak of the devil. After greeting the girls, she walked toward Matt and swallowed her pride. "Hi."

Blue eyes skimmed over her as though he was checking to see if she was packing a gun. "Are you officially talking to me now? In public?"

"Maybe."

"I'm glad. I've had a heck of a day."

Immediately, concern overcame resentment. "What happened?"

"Too much to talk about here."

"But maybe someplace else?"

"Yes…if you're not afraid to be seen with me."

"Uh-oh. Things are bad?"

"Hell, yes. Well, until I came in here."

There it was, humor filtering on through, warming her up and making her feel that Newton's laws of attraction had nothing on the sparks that flew between her and Matt. "Did I ever thank you for your help with Kimber? If you hadn't shown up, I don't know if I would have ever gotten her out of that bathroom."

"It wasn't any big deal. I think she was mostly worried about George."

"So is there any particular reason you came in?"

"Yes, as a matter of fact." Matt slid his hands in the back pockets of his jeans. Against her will, Minnie watched the action, then turned away as she realized two of the girls were watching those hands, too. Yep, Matt Madigan could surely fill out a pair of jeans like nobody's business.

After she directed him out of the girls' line of vision, Matt lifted a hand and rested it on the card rack next to her. Boxing her in.

Years ago, Minnie would have noticed just how tall and strong Matt was, so up close and personal. But not any longer. Oh, no. No longer was she the type of girl who got taken in by a pair of blue eyes and a real good backside. "Do…you need a card?"

"Not a one."

"Gift?"

"Nope." Leaning closer, Matt murmured, "I was hoping you might call a truce to our feuding and stop over later tonight. We got a mess of peaches at the farmers' market this afternoon."

"I love peaches."

"Mrs. Wy told me to tell you and Kimber that she was making a pound cake to go with them. We bought ice cream, too."

"It sounds like a feast."

"It's going to be good, and that's a fact. So will you make Mrs. Wy happy and say yes? She asked that I come over here and ask you special."

"That's nice of you to do that for Wanda."

"Oh, hell, Minnie. You know I want you there, too. I hate looking out my front door and being afraid to see you glaring at me across the way."

She didn't appreciate how that sounded. "Glaring?"

"Fuming?" He leaned even closer. So close that their lips could meet if she wasn't standing as still as a statue. "Minnie, say yes. Even if you won't find the company great, I can promise the food will be."

The way to a girl's heart should not be through her stomach. *Really.* But Wanda made a pound cake that could melt in your mouth. And, well, Kimber would love being near Matt and Wanda. "What time should we stop by?"

"You'll come?"

"I don't want to disappoint Kimber or Wanda."

"What about me? Aren't you worried about disappointing me?" Oh, his voice had lowered a bit, sounding gravelly. Almost sexy.

She glanced at his lips. Wondered what it would feel like to kiss him. Really kiss him.

He grinned slowly.

Suddenly it hit her. Matt knew exactly what he was doing. He knew she had a weak spot for him that had nothing to do with pound cake and everything to do with a crush that didn't have the decency to go away.

She fought to remain aloof. To remember that his company was about to put hers out of business. "Not particularly. After all, you are my competition."

He stepped back. "Minnie Clark, I can't help it if you don't like my job. Don't be mad at me forever."

"I'm not mad, and I did apologize. I'm just stronger and wiser now."

"You still sound peeved."

Minnie caught the girls watching and, for a moment, she considered flirting outrageously with Matt, just to let them know that Minnie Clark could have a chance with Crescent View's most favored son.

Thank goodness she didn't think of him in those terms. Not anymore. "What time should we stop by?" she asked again.

"Seven?"

"Seven's good. Please tell Wanda thank you."

"I'll do that." He pivoted on his heel, and just about ran into the trio of girls who'd been edging close enough to smell his aftershave.

Every one of them was standing perky and pretty,

peering at him with love-struck expressions. After a second of gawking, one stepped forward. "Hey."

"Hi, there." Matt looked completely uncomfortable. Minnie noticed that he was having a real hard time figuring out where to look, too. At the moment, his eyes seemed fixated on a spot just to the left of the girls, inches from the door.

Minnie took pity on him. "Girls, step aside, please. Mr. Madigan can't get out with y'all blocking the door."

They stepped, but not without another stream of giggles and Matt very debonairly tipping his ball cap. When the door chimed his exit, the whole crew scurried forward, each holding a handful of cards, gel pens and beaded bracelets. "Who was that, Minnie?" one asked.

"Matt Madigan. He used to live here."

"Where does he live now?"

Minnie claimed the first girl's items and began ringing them up. "Actually, he's moving into Mrs. Wyzecki's place."

In unison, the girls turned around to watch Matt through the window. He was visiting with a pair of elderly men on the sidewalk. With the sun shining on him, Matt Madigan looked shiny. Larger-than-life.

A pretty blonde sighed. "He's so handsome. Well, for someone so old."

Finally, Minnie's smile felt genuine. "He is old. Real old." She pushed the paper sack forward. "That'll be nine dollars, please."

MINNIE CLARK NEEDED to settle down and step off her high horse, Matt decided as he walked out to his F-150. Shoot, the way she'd been talking and fussing, you'd think he was an ax murderer hunting for a new victim.

He was just trying to make a living, just like she was. It wasn't his fault that the two jobs might lock horns every once in a while.

Of course, as he reviewed the conversation he'd just had with Abel Pierce, Matt knew Minnie wasn't the only one who felt that way. Abel had heard about the new bidding requests and had taken it upon himself to tell Matt what he thought about that.

When he entered Mrs. Wy's, he found her slicing peaches in the kitchen. She looked a little flushed. "Mrs. Wy, you okay?"

"I'm fine. It's just hot as blazes out."

The kitchen felt a cool seventy degrees. "Not in here." Worried that she'd been moving furniture or stacks of boxes around without him, he asked, "What have you been doing all afternoon?"

"Just this and that. I sorted through Jim's closet for a bit, but then decided to take a break."

"You sure you feel okay? You don't look too good."

"I'm fine." With a weak smile, she said, "I guess all this packing has taken it out of me."

Instantly he put his problems aside. This is what he should be worrying about—how to make Mrs. Wy's transition and move as easy as possible. He set the ice cream on the counter and gently removed the knife from her hands. "Tough, huh?"

In an instant, Mrs. Wy reached out to him. "Real tough. I'm having a hard time throwing so much away, Matt. I feel like I'm just supposed to toss forty years away in ten minutes."

Relieved that she wasn't ill, just feeling over-whelmed, he helped her to her favorite chair. "How about I call one of those storage places? We can put all those things you don't want to part with there."

"What am I going to do then, Matt? Go to a shed to look at my life?"

She sounded more depressed than Matt could ever recall her being. "Mrs. Wy, how about you sip some tea while I cook us up some dinner?"

"You can do that?"

"I can grill. Hey, steaks sound good?"

She slowly lifted herself onto a stool. "I suppose."

"You're going to make me feel bad, acting so indifferent."

"I'd hate to do that." Little by little color filled her cheeks. "How did it go with Minnie?"

"She's still not real crazy about me."

"Give her time. She's got a lot on her plate. That Kimber would make a weaker person get the shakes."

Matt laughed at that. Remembering the great bathroom-guinea pig debate through the bathroom door, he said, "Kimber would have done me in some time ago."

Looking off to somewhere private, Mrs. Wy murmured, "Losing someone you love is hard. And the pain comes back to bite you when you don't expect it. I'm having a hard time at seventy-four. Don't know how a little girl is holding up so well."

Matt knew. Though the pain from losing his parents had long since dimmed, he knew that getting through the terrible haze of grief was a painful and long journey. "She'll make it. She has Minnie. And Minnie has a way about her that's pretty special."

"She does at that. So are those young ladies coming over for peaches and pound cake?"

"Minnie said she would." Matt didn't see the need to

share that getting her to agree hadn't been the easiest task in the world.

"Then she will. Minnie always does what she says she will. Always."

"I don't know what to do about her. I wanted SavNGo to come to this town to help it, not put small business owners out of business."

"Owners? Are other people upset, too?"

"Yeah. Maybe. I spoke to some men outside of Minnie's place. They'd just come from the hardware store and were kind of grilling me about different things." Matt moved his neck around, tried to get it loosened up. "I got the impression they're feeling torn…like they wouldn't mind paying less for things, but don't want to stop giving people they like their business. I…can't say I blame them."

"If you didn't bring SavNGo here, someone else would have. Things change, Matthew. Small towns either prosper or whither and die. People adjust to losses and become stronger—or bitter. Minnie and Abel will come up with something."

"I'm sure you're right."

"I know I am. Minnie's stronger than she looks. Peter's leaving hit her hard. But don't worry, Matthew. It's not like you can switch jobs. Minnie will come around sooner or later. She's never been able to hold a grudge for long."

Matt hoped Mrs. Wy was right about that.

Chapter Nine

The peaches were awfully good. Firm, not too juicy, sweet enough by themselves for dessert, but truly decadent when paired with ice cream and rich, buttery cake. Minnie, Wanda, Kimber and Matt had been sitting around the cereal bar eating for a good ten minutes.

Already it felt like an eternity. All Minnie saw when she looked at Matt was her store imploding while his precious SavNGo loomed in the distance.

But since he wasn't going anywhere, maybe it was time to do a little more thinking about what she could do to help herself and a little less feeling sorry for her circumstances.

She made a mental note to plan another meeting with Brenda and Abel. If they put their minds to it, Minnie was sure they could come up with some good ideas about how to save their businesses.

In the meantime, Minnie did her best to remain cordial but cool, which was kind of hard, considering Matt had changed into a fresh pair of jeans and a snug white T-shirt. No man should look so good.

Kimber was also vying for the position of his new

best friend and Matt—thank goodness—was giving her all the patience and love the little girl deserved.

Minnie felt as if she were walking on a tightrope, balancing between thankfulness that her niece was finally coming out of her shell and resentment that Matt Madigan—of all people!—was the one who'd inspired the change.

So far the big dessert party had lasted thirty minutes. Surely in another ten or so she and Kimber could leave. Desperate for conversation, Minnie turned to Wanda. "How's the packing going?"

"Not so good." Wanda blinked as tears welled up in her eyes. "I got into Jim's closet and couldn't seem to step out of the past. I'm not sure if I can give any of his things away."

Oops. Wrong conversation starter. "I imagine that would be hard."

Kimber glared at Minnie. "We had to give all of my Mommy and Daddy's things away. Before we moved here."

Matt raised a brow. Minnie didn't correct the girl. But that wasn't quite how the moving and packing had gone. It had been more of a terrible production, looking at all of Paige and Jeremy's things and trying to figure out what she should save for Kimber one day and what should be best left forgotten.

Her parents had been too wrapped up in their grief to give much direction. Jeremy's mother had been slightly better but unable to make any decisions. Ultimately, Minnie had decided to rent a storage room and put an assortment of items inside. One day Kimber and her grandparents could go through it all.

Slipping a hand on Kimber's shoulder, Wanda whispered, "Want to go watch baseball? The Rangers are on. They're playing the Indians this evening."

With one more spiteful glare in Minnie's direction, Kimber nodded. "Uh-huh."

Off they went, leaving Minnie alone with Matt. *Shoot.*

Matt winked at Minnie, as if they weren't almost enemies. "Mrs. Wy's making a big deal out of that game because she knows it just about drives me crazy." He called out, "The way you talk, Mrs. Wy, you'd think I forgotten all about the Rangers."

"I think you did!"

"The Rangers will always be my team."

"Humph. You seemed to embrace those Phillies easily enough. Kimber and I'll give you an update during the next commercial," Wanda said as she and the little girl hopped up on the reclining love seat and clicked on the remote.

That settled, Matt and Minnie made quick work of the dishes, neatly stacking each bowl in the rack to the side of the stainless steel sink.

Minnie was too aware of Matt once again. Her emotions were on high alert and Minnie knew it wouldn't take much to either hit Matt or grab him close and kiss him, fast and furious.

It was definitely time to leave. "Do you want to go watch the game? I could head on home and give you some peace."

"I'll watch later." He motioned to the porch. "How about we go sit outside for a bit? The humidity's not too tough this time of night."

"I don't think—"

"Please, Min? I'd like to speak with you. Privately."

After seeing that Kimber couldn't be more comfortable in the living room, Minnie reluctantly gave in. "Fine."

Feeling as if she were going to an execution, she plodded along after Matt, stepping through the front door, and almost welcoming the blast of hot air that greeted them. As crickets chirped a squawky welcome, Matt sat down on an ancient white wicker love seat. Wisely, Minnie picked the top step of the stoop. There was no way she was going to sit next to him.

Matt noticed. "You worried I'll bite?"

Biting made her think of his lips which, once upon a time, she'd thought an awful lot about being on hers. "No. There's more space over here."

After a pause, he said, "You know, I didn't come back to Crescent View to make you miserable. I'm not trying to make anyone miserable."

"You're not." She was doing just fine on her own. Minnie knew it wasn't Matt's fault that she found she was still attracted to him, or that her little business was going to be in trouble because of SavNGo's good fortunes. "I heard y'all broke ground today."

He visibly winced. "We don't have to talk about work, do we?"

"It's why you're here."

"Not the only reason. And it's certainly not why I wanted to talk to you."

"What did you want to say?"

"I'd like for us to be friends again."

Minnie tried to play it cool. "*Again?* Matt Madigan, I don't know if we've ever gotten beyond the acquaintance stage."

"That's kind of a shame, don't you think?"

"Why? There's no reason for us to be anything more."

"Come now, Min. We do have some ties. After all, I did date your sister."

"That and fifty cents will buy you a cup of coffee. *Everyone* dated my sister."

"Ouch."

A brush of conscience made Minnie feel guilty. "I'm taking back that last part."

"Paige didn't date everyone?"

"Paige did, but I shouldn't hold it against her." For a moment, Minnie smiled in surprise. It was the first time she'd actually said Paige's name without feeling the usual all-encompassing wave of grief.

Matt hopped off the wicker chair and joined her on the stoop. "Come on, Min," he murmured. "Stop making this so tough. I did help you with Kimber in the bathroom."

And because Minnie couldn't help herself—or didn't want to—she finally gave in. "I guess we could be acquaintances."

"Come, now."

"All right. Friends."

"I'll take that." For once, Matt looked completely, utterly serious. "See, Min, I could sure use a friend right now. Lane's mad at me. Other people are, too. Fact is, putting up this store is causing a bit more commotion than I ever realized."

He continued before she could think of a thing to say. "I trust you, Minnie. Mrs. Wy's getting older. Before I know it, she'll have finished moving out and be in her fancy retirement community."

"And you'll be here."

But instead of flashing her the wicked grin she expected, Matt just looked even more despondent. "I will, and truth be told, I don't rightly know how I feel about that. Mrs. Wy's my only real link to the past."

"That's not true. You've got a lot of good friends."

"But only one person who actually loves me. I need a friend." Leaning closer, he said, "If we don't discuss our work too much, I have a strong feeling that we could come up with a whole lot of other things to talk about. What do you think? Are you willing to give that a try?"

Minnie felt her mouth go as dry as the sands of the Sahara. Well, at least as dry as it used to right before she was about to go into her final exams. Matt had that effect on her, made her excited and giddy and doubtful about herself.

Insecure and thrilled to be noticed.

At the moment, those murky blue eyes were gazing into hers, creating a sweet spell of nostalgia and old-fashioned lust, right there on Wanda's front porch. This conversation was the stuff of dreams and nightmares all rolled up into one.

And the sad, sad truth of it was Minnie wasn't sure which feeling was which. But, there, as the moon started rising and the first star of the night blinked on, she cast a look in Matt's eyes and deep down realized that she was being given an opportunity to be in the company of the one man she'd always admired. She could let work problems interfere or not.

It was too late to pretend things hadn't happened that had. And he wasn't the poster child for progress in north Texas. No, he was just a man with a really good job. It was time to face facts.

Even if Matt hadn't come out to see Wanda, SaveNGo or some other big chain was due to come to town.

Even if he wasn't there, she would be worrying about the future of her store.

Even if Matt wasn't living across the street or sitting right there next to her, she'd still find herself waking up every once in a blue moon and remembering. Remember how attractive he'd been. Remember how much she'd coveted his attention. How she'd been unable to take her eyes off him when he'd been all suited up for football.

No matter what their circumstances were now, Minnie knew there would have to come a time when she would have thought about Matt Madigan and wondered all about what could have been. If things had been different.

Now she didn't have to.

Shoot. Was she really going to let herself go down that road again? To sit around thinking about what might have been? Go to sleep thinking about dreams and wishes? "I think we could have a lot to talk about," she said softly. "If we didn't talk about business."

"I know we could."

"And Kimber—she thinks you're great."

"The feeling's mutual. She thinks you're great, too."

"I don't know about that. We had some rough times...."

"I do. She loves you."

Minnie turned and looked at him. Really looked, not just at the idea of the man, but the actual one sitting right next to her.

Pensive and solemn, he stared back. "We going to be okay?"

"I think so."

"Good." In a flash, that trademark confidence returned tenfold. Minnie didn't know how he did it, but Matt seemed to emanate even more of a swagger and sex appeal than before. His legs stretched out in front of him, showing just how much of that six-foot-two height was encased in faded denim.

As the tension between them increased, Matt obviously waiting for her to talk, Minnie chuckled. "I'm so used to being irritated at you, at the moment I can't think of anything to say."

"I can." Scooting a little closer, he murmured, "Let's start with you, Minnie Clark. How'd you get so gorgeous?"

Time stood still as the words sank in.

Then anger reared up and smacked her in the face. The question—the obvious ridiculousness of it—made her seethe. She wasn't gorgeous. And that silly old line, spoken just as smoothly as softened butter, grated on her like nobody's business.

Standing up, she put some distance between them. "This was a big mistake. I'm going to go get Kimber and leave."

His legs shifted back under him. "Huh? Why? Minnie, what the hell did I say?"

"Nothing good."

"Hold, now." Blue eyes widened. "Was it my compliment?"

If she wasn't so embarrassed, she would have socked him one. She made do by standing up.

He stood, too, then stopped her in her tracks by grabbing her hand. "I'm sorry."

"For what, Matt?"

"For being attracted to you, okay?" Still gazing at her lips, he murmured, "Don't be mad."

"I'm not," she whispered. Then wondered what he would say if he really knew the truth—that she'd never slept with a man, that she was a virgin. He'd probably take back every word he'd just said.

Chapter Ten

Matt's BlackBerry kept beeping and buzzing on his hip. If he didn't move the holder, he was half afraid he was going to get some kind of electrical charge in a place that could do serious damage.

But that was the least of his worries. Ever since he'd had to tell the subcontractors that they'd need to rebid, he'd lost what little free time he had. Phone calls and e-mails were being exchanged between himself, corporate and all the new people who wanted to bid.

He'd been helping to pack in the afternoons, which meant he was working far too late. He was exhausted. He'd give a lot for just a few moments' peace.

So far that hadn't happened. When the darn Black-Berry wasn't buzzing, his cell phone was. And when neither were doing their thing, he was receiving yet more e-mails, or had a meeting to take care of.

"Yeah?" he barked as he stood in front of the window in his room and noticed that Minnie's shades were open. Sunlight seemed to bounce off her windowpanes, making the glass look sparkly. Like she was greeting the new day shiny and bright. "Madigan."

"Hey, Matt. Catch you at a bad time?"

Matt drew a steadying breath. "Hey, Jackie. Sorry I snapped at you." She'd been with him for four years. All five feet of her could snap him into place with a well-chosen glare. And she was as loyal as the day was long. She sure didn't need any attitude from him. "What do you need?"

"Oh…everything." Her voice as sassy as ever, she continued talking at her usual trademark fast-as-a-fire-cracker clip. "You missed a conference call last night."

"Oops."

"I could think of more choice words than that, especially since I was the lucky person who was chosen to fill you in." As she paused for breath, Matt heard a *tap-tap-tap* on the keyboard in front of her. "You still working at SavNGo, Matt, or did you resign and forget to tell me?"

"Ha-ha. You know I've been working nonstop."

"Except last night."

Matt knew he'd been out of sorts since his big admittance to Minnie, which had gone over as well as a balloon filled with lead. How could he have been such a fool and get all soft and emotional with her?

"Settle down." Matt strode over to his laptop, which was perched on an ancient green vinyl card table right next to the bed. With a few buttons, he found his calendar, then noticed that he had, indeed, missed last night's conference call. It had been at seven his time, five in California. He'd been eating peaches with Minnie. "I forgot about the call."

"You forgot?"

Matt couldn't blame Jackie's shock. At work, back in Philly, he worked 24/7. Since he didn't have any close relationships, they didn't interfere with business. And since they were rolling out four and five stores a year, there was always business to concentrate on. "Last night we got busy with peaches and ice cream and I forgot about the time."

As Jackie started flipping pages and spouting numbers, old habits and his work ethic kicked in. For the next twenty minutes he wrote down notes, scanned incoming e-mails and did his best to keep on track.

"Matt, I was thinking that maybe I should come out for a bit and give you a hand. I know all this paperwork with the bids has got to be a nightmare."

Jackie was an outstanding assistant. She was also forceful and had a helluva figure. She was even more motivated than he was for a big promotion.

Actually, her presence would most likely set him straight, as well as everyone around. "I could use your help, Jack, but I'm not sure where you could stay. The closest motel is a good thirty minutes away."

"How about at your place?"

Matt wasn't sure how that would go over. "Jackie, I don't know about that. What if word got back to corporate? We both know you've got a promotion in mind. I sure wouldn't want anyone thinking we weren't acting any way other than professional."

"Matt, why don't you let me worry about my reputation? I haven't been putting in sixty hour work weeks for nothing, you know."

This wasn't their usual topic of conversation. In four years they'd maybe had one or two discussions not business related, and those had been about traffic conditions during a snowstorm. "Any chance you want to tell me what's going on? What's really going on?"

"If you must know, I'm having boyfriend troubles. Keith broke up with me."

He'd never really thought about Jackie having a social life. "Sorry to hear about that."

"He said I worked too much." She paused. "Please, Matt? I need to get out of here for a little bit."

Other women would ask for a vacation. Jackie asked to go to north Texas. "If you want to meet me here, I'd really appreciate it. And you can stay here, too. We'll just make sure everyone knows there's nothing between us."

Jackie chuckled. "Thanks."

"You're welcome."

"I'll go make reservations right now," she said, sounding more like her usual self again. "I'll call you later."

Thinking of Jackie with a man made him think of Minnie, which in turn made him stand up and turn to the window again.

Just like a stalker.

Damn. During the time he'd been on the phone, Minnie had gotten a visitor. At the moment, she was standing outside talking to some guy in a pair of khakis and a bright tomato-colored golf shirt. Bracing a palm on his windowpane, Matt struggled to see if the guy looked familiar. He didn't.

Who the hell was he?

But all he really wanted to do was spy on Minnie, which was a treat. She looked pretty. Her thick brown hair hung down past her shoulder blades. She had on a flirty denim skirt and a lacy kind of tank top.

Hold on, there!

That lace top was kind of low cut and peachy-colored. Silky, too. From here it almost looked like Minnie Clark was standing outside in just a slip of lingerie.

Boy, did she look a sight! From his vantage point,

with the sun streaming down on her, making her lacy top all shimmery, she was mesmerizing. No doubt about it, Minnie had the kind of figure men dreamed about. She filled a top out real nice. And her skin was so soft-looking it made him think about holding her close and feeling those generous curves.

Added to it all was a whiff of wholesomeness... mixing with Mrs. Wy's warning that not a lot of men had gotten real close.

Matt knew he'd spoken the wrong way when he'd blurted an old practiced line about how she was gorgeous. Mrs. Wy had hinted more than once that Minnie wasn't a real knowledgeable woman. Innocent-like.

Matt scowled as he noticed that her visitor was having a difficult time looking away from all that skin Minnie was showing off.

Didn't Minnie see the commotion she was causing? Someone really ought to give her a talking-to about dressing a bit more modestly.

The BlackBerry buzzed. He scanned the incoming messages, but really, his heart wasn't in it.

Who was that guy?

Luckily Mrs. Wy called up to him and broke his spell. "Matthew? You busy?"

"No, ma'am." With relief, he put the BlackBerry down. "I'll be right there." He walked downstairs to find Mrs. Wy staring out the front window, too, shaking her head. "What's going on?"

"I thought we'd tackle the study today," she said, but she didn't sound too excited about it. In fact, she just sounded preoccupied. Kind of the way he felt.

"The study sounds good." Even though he knew, he said, "What are you looking at?"

She pursed her lips. "Minnie."

Glad to get things out in the open, he said, "I saw her from my window upstairs. Who's that she's with?"

"Peter."

"That's Minnie's ex-boyfriend?"

"None other." Mrs. Wy turned from the window and looked his way. "I guess Peter couldn't stay away from Crescent View, either."

PETER HAD JUST ABOUT GIVEN Minnie a heart attack. When she'd heard the bell, followed by an impatient knock, she'd answered the door, thinking to greet Matt. Anxious to go back to their now constant war of words, which was strangely exhilarating and more fun than she'd ever admit out loud.

But instead of her new neighbor, there was Peter Ross on the other side of her oak door. Before she could do a thing, he'd gripped her hand and pulled her outside.

She'd gone willingly because she didn't want him in her house. Come to think of it, she didn't want Peter to see a trace of Kimber, especially since he'd clearly stated that he didn't want anything to do with her.

Minnie wasn't too thrilled about being anywhere near Peter, either. Especially not when he was acting as if there was something special between them. She knew that there was most definitely not. Not anymore. "Why are you here?"

"I wanted to see you." Something in his eyes glinted, indicating doublespeak.

She didn't care for that.

When he tried to reach for her hand again, she slapped it away. "I don't know why you stopped by here at all. We don't have a thing to say to each other."

Thin lips pressed together, making her wonder how she'd ever kissed him. Kissed him so much!

Next, as she eyed his smooth good looks and his ugly designer shirt, Minnie also seriously wondered why she'd ever considered spending the rest of her life with him. She must have been suffering from temporary insanity.

Peter sat down in one of her pretty white rocking chairs uninvited, then had the nerve to offer her a seat, too. She sat but couldn't help glaring at him as she did so.

He noticed. "Why are you being like this, Min?"

"If you're talking about my being less than welcoming, it probably has something to do with the fact that I don't want to see you. You broke up with me, remember? You need to get on home."

Instead of listening, Peter leaned back, forcing the bottom rung of the rocker to stick the front part out. He stayed there, immobile. Resting his elbows on the armrests, he started talking. "*Home* is up in the air, if you want to know the truth."

"Oh?"

"See, Dallas wasn't like I thought it was going to be. Selling copiers was even harder than I thought."

"I'm really not interested in hearing this story."

As she expected, he ignored her wishes and droned on. "I had to get to work every morning at eight and the commute took a full hour from my apartment, so that meant I was up at six. When I'd finally get to work, I had to sign in and go to a meeting. Then after listening to a bunch of people tell me how I had to make my numbers, I had to go out and try to get appointments."

Peter stared at her, his eyes full of disappointment.

"You'd be surprised at the number of people who don't want a copier, Min."

Against her will, she was sucked in. "So you gave up?"

He straightened, which made the rocker on his chair swing into action. He shifted. "I did not give up. I was fired."

She did not want to feel sorry for him. She really did not. She needed to focus on the negatives, the things that drove her nuts whenever she thought about him. "What about all the other women?"

His head popped up. "What other women?"

"The women I was holding you back from. The women you wanted to meet." Minnie recalled every stinking minute of their breakup conversation. Every little reason Peter had given her for his departure. "You were going to find someone experienced." As in the complete opposite of her. "Don't you remember?"

He flushed. "If you're hoping I got something coming, you don't have to worry. I got my just deserts, and then some. The women in Big D weren't looking too hard for a small-town guy, I'm afraid."

"Peter, you're not hoping to start up with me again, are you?" She felt her cheeks burning with embarrassment. "Because things haven't changed. I still have Kimber. I'll always have her, and I don't want it any other way."

"You know, I never really got to know her. Maybe we could start over."

Like that was going to make everything better. Just the thought of putting her niece around a man like him made her sick.

"I can't believe you'd think I'd subject her to you again. Have you lost your mind?"

"Maybe. Maybe I've been so lost that I can't see

straight anymore." He reached for her. "Let's give it another shot, Min."

She moved out of his reach. "No."

"Come on. What we had was good, Minnie. It just took some time apart for me to see that. To *recognize* that."

"Well, I took our little time apart to realize that I don't want you anymore."

"Who else are you going to get?"

Against her will, Minnie's gaze strayed to Matt, who'd just come out onto Wanda's front porch and was sipping coffee from an oversize mug and making no secret that he was watching them.

Peter turned to look at Matt, too, then whipped his head back to Minnie's. "You've gotta be kidding me. You're not eyeing *him* now, are you?"

She didn't know what irritated her more—Peter's attitude or his careless words. She stood up. "What's wrong with him?"

Peter rose, too, and used the opportunity to step a little closer. "Look at that tricked-up truck. Those boots. I see his looks. I know his type. I know he's not ever going to go after a girl like you."

"A girl like me?"

"Come on, Min. You told me yourself that you were inexperienced. If you got yourself out of your Jane Austen mode, you'd realize that guys don't look for prudes anymore. Especially not men like him."

Minnie looked at Matt again. Catching her eye, he lifted his mug in greeting and smiled. Oh, that grin, full of white teeth and temptation. Unable to stop herself, she gave a little wave back.

Peter scowled. "You're making a fool of yourself."

"I am definitely not. Matt Madigan and I are friends."

"Matt Madigan? Hey, I've heard of him." Minnie could practically see his brain whirling. "He went to high school here, didn't he?"

"He did."

"Oh, my gosh." Peter's face flushed. "Wasn't he all-American or something?"

Minnie raised her chin, as though she'd had something to do with it. "He was."

Peter started laughing. "That's why I like you, Minnie. Ever so dreamy, your head always in the clouds."

"Hey, Minnie."

Oh, Lord. Matt Madigan had once again decided to go where he wasn't welcome and saunter on over. And he'd heard Peter's comment.

As he stood there on her lawn, as patient as you please, Minnie knew she had no choice but to make some introductions. "Peter Ross, please meet Matt Madigan."

Matt stepped up on her porch, then held out his hand to Peter in a friendly manner.

Grudgingly, Peter returned the handshake. "Hello."

Minnie didn't know what to say. Helplessly she looked from Matt, her nemesis in business, to Peter, the man who'd formerly broken her heart but now she wished she'd run over with a steamroller.

Matt glanced at his watch then at her, giving her the kind of look that said everything between them was good and wonderful. "Minnie, honey, please tell me you haven't forgotten about our lunch date today."

Her eyes widened, and she was about to tell him she wasn't intending to ever have lunch with him except that Peter let out a grunt. A grunt!

Well, that made her mad enough to play along. "I haven't forgotten."

"Good, 'cause I've been counting the hours." He had the grace to try to look embarrassed. Embarrassed! Him, Matt Madigan! "That's why I came tromping on over here. I couldn't stay away."

Matt moved closer, stepping right in between her and Peter. Next thing she knew, Matt reached out and took her hand and folded five fingers over hers in a definite show of ownership. Behind Matt's shoulder, Peter narrowed his eyes.

Minnie let herself be tugged closer. Close enough to feel the fabric of his Levi's rub against her skirt. Close enough to see that he hadn't shaved yet and that he smelled faintly of Ivory soap and extrastrong coffee.

Looking over his shoulder, Matt murmured, "You mind excusing us for a sec? I mean, your conversation's done, right?"

"It's over," Minnie said.

Peter descended the front steps. Then paused. "Minnie, we still need to talk."

Oh, no, they most certainly did not! "Bye, Peter."

"But—"

This time it was Matt who turned and glared. "Watch your step on the way out."

"Huh? Oh, sure." Slowly Peter walked to his Taurus. Minnie noticed he turned their way every couple of seconds.

She and Matt were still holding hands. Still standing close. So close she could see that a faint line of perspiration had formed at the neck of Matt's shirt.

Peter's car door opened and slammed shut. When they were finally alone, Minnie said, "Thanks for coming over here."

"No problem."

"Peter has a bad habit of spouting off things."

His jaw jumped. "So I heard."

"Oh. Well—"

He rolled his eyes. "That guy's a piece of work, Min. I would have thought you'd have better taste in men."

"I usually do." In the distance she heard the Taurus's engine turn on, but Peter didn't shift into gear. Minnie leaned a little closer. "Why do you think Peter hasn't driven off?"

Matt gave her a look that said the answer was obvious. "He's waiting."

"For what?"

"For this." And then Matt Madigan finally did the stuff of her teenage-girl dreams.

He kissed her.

Very slowly, very deliberately. Yep, those lips of his, those so firm, so perfect, so Matt lips planted themselves on hers and settled in.

Her knees turned to mush. Minnie raised her free hand and gripped his shoulder for support. Matt wrapped his hands around her waist. Immediately, warmth seeped through the silky material and made her tingly all over.

Then, much to her surprise, he turned his head a bit and kissed her some more.

Lord have mercy. Minnie held on and opened her lips. Invited his tongue. Tasted Matt. Tasted everything she'd ever imagined.

She was almost oblivious when Peter Ross and his old tan Taurus finally popped into gear and drove out of sight.

Chapter Eleven

"Why'd you do that?"

Matt inhaled a deep breath of air and looked into Minnie's chocolate eyes. "You know why. You needed kissing."

"To make Peter jealous?"

He placed a hand back on her waist, enjoying the feeling of it not being all hard and bony. Instead, it was soft and curvy. Completely different from his own. He liked that. "I don't know if I kissed you only to make that jerk jealous, Min. I do know that I don't like hearing him talk to you as if you're lacking something. Because you're not."

What he did feel, and wasn't in any hurry to tell her, was that he'd kissed her because he'd had the opportunity and he'd taken it.

He had a lot of faults, but waiting for things was never his style.

Uncertainty filled her gaze. Minnie lifted her left hand and placed it on his shoulder. Squeezed a bit, like she needed to get her bearings. "I can't believe he came back."

He'd been raised without a mother, but even he knew better than to tell a girl she wasn't good enough.

And Minnie, well, she had a lot of charms.

But he knew he couldn't just ignore her problems. He also couldn't ignore how nice it felt to be touching her this way. And how comfortable she seemed to be touching him, too. Not wanting to let her go, he fastened his other hand on her other hip and pulled her a little closer. "We're all coming back out of the woodwork, just to see you," he said, coaxing a smile from her.

She was shocked at his bold words, and a hearty laugh erupted from her. "Matt, you say the darnedest things."

"He's not worth your time of day, Min. We both know that. You were terrific, giving him his walking papers."

"I don't know about that. I guess he failed other places, so he thought he could win with me." She shook her head in wonder. "I can't believe how he assumed that I'd welcome him back."

"You sure didn't do that."

"No." She tilted up her chin. "I'm kind of proud of myself."

"I'm proud of you, too."

Shaking her head, she looked beyond him, at Mrs. Wy's front porch. "For a moment I almost felt sorry for him, and then he started talking about you."

"Me?"

"Once he found out who you were, he acted like I'd never have a shot with you." Minnie stiffened for a moment. "Shoot. Sorry, I didn't mean for it to sound like I was after you. It's just that, gosh, for him, once a quarterback, always a quarterback. And since I wasn't cheerleader-perfect, I would never have a chance with you." Under her breath, she murmured, "I'm so glad I never slept with him."

She hadn't slept with her almost-fiancé? Now that

was news. When she looked at him with all kinds of embarrassment, he asked the obvious. "Why didn't you?"

"I, uh, have been waiting."

Quietly, he said, "All this time?"

She rolled her eyes as her cheeks flushed. "I absolutely *cannot* believe I'm telling you this. But, yeah."

"That's smart, don't you think?"

"Do you?"

"Definitely."

Matt could feel her relax underneath his hands. She stepped a little closer and, to his great surprise, rested her forehead on his shoulder. Then her shoulders started shaking.

Alarm coursed through him. "Min?"

"I wish I could have seen his eyes when you put your arms around me. Told me you couldn't wait for lunch."

She was laughing.

He started chuckling, too. Everything with work and the move had been so stressful, the release of laughter was welcome. After brushing a kiss to her brow, he smoothed down her hair along her back, enjoying the fine, silky texture.

He'd never been a guy to care whether a woman had long or short hair. As long as it was pretty, he didn't care. But something pulled inside of him, and he knew he'd be sad if she cut it all off. There was something about her long hair and curvy figure that felt so right to him…that struck him as pretty and perfect.

Almost as quickly as it started, the laughter stopped. She tilted her head back. He stared at her lips. They parted.

And he kissed her again.

This time, now that they didn't have an audience and all, things were a little different. Minnie responded to him, curved into him. Made him feel ten feet tall and all muscle.

Made him feel like the guy he used to be, back when he was quarterback and his social calendar was full even though his home life sucked. He pulled her closer, felt those breasts so scantily covered in silk rub against his shirt. His body sprang to life.

Next thing he knew, he was sitting on a wicker seat, pulling her onto his lap, just so he could feel her in his arms. That soft cool skin. Sweet and pliant. Tempting him in ways he hadn't been tempted in quite some time.

Abruptly, she pulled away. Jumped up. Shocked. "Oh my gosh." Her eyes widened as she looked down and saw that her top was twisted and half her bra was peeking out. "I'm going to go on in. Now."

He'd scared her. Had he scared her? "Wait a minute. Don't you think we ought to talk or something?" Though what in the world were they going to talk about? How he really liked kissing her? How he knew she didn't have a lot of experience but he found that endearing, not a turnoff?

Yeah, that would really get her to relax.

"Min—"

"Thanks for coming over. For helping me out with Peter. For kissing me."

He shook his head, appalled. "Don't thank me for kissing you." Because she still looked doubtful, he grabbed at her hand and held on when she attempted to pull it away. "I meant it, Min. I liked kissing you."

If anything, that seemed to make Minnie more flustered. "I gotta go. You better go. Bye, Matt."

And with that, her door opened and shut, and Matt walked slowly on back to Mrs. Wyzecki's house. Why had he gone and kissed Minnie like that? Why was he now thinking about first times and innocence and how sweet her arms had felt, wrapped around his neck?

Why? Why? Why?

Chapter Twelve

Wanda Wyzecki showed up at Carried Away with her tennis shoes on and a color brochure of Shady Glen Retirement Community. "Minnie, I need to pick out colors for my new place. Can you help me? That is, if you don't already have plans."

"Of course I can. The store's been worse than quiet all afternoon. Want to get some tea and sit under one of the park's awnings?"

"I was just going to suggest that. So…are you sure you don't have any plans? Word is that you've been kissing Matt Madigan on your front porch."

"Maybe color swatches aren't all you're thinking about, Wanda."

"This time the gossip concerns two of my favorite people. Time I got the facts, don't you know. I saw Matt go out to speak with you, but then I went to get my hair done. While I was sitting under the dryer, I heard Zenia and Cora Jean Hardt gossiping away…about you two. Cora Jean drove by and spied the two of you on your front porch."

Minnie took a moment to admire Wanda's hair before replying. "There's not much to say, not really."

Other than that kiss had been nice.

Real nice.

Minnie had felt pretty and special in Matt's arms. And, well, he'd smelled good. Like fresh soap and sporty aftershave. His body had felt solid and muscular under his white T-shirt, and the way his hands had curved around her rear had made her think that she had a nice figure. That maybe she wasn't too big, after all.

In short, kissing Matt Madigan was the stuff that dreams were made of. The stuff that her dreams had always been made of, and truth be told, Minnie wasn't real sure what to think about having the reality be as good as her fantasies.

Surely that wasn't supposed to be how it was?

Seeing that it wasn't too crowded, and that April had everything under control, Minnie went ahead and pulled off her apron. "Let me go tell April that I'm taking a break, then I'll meet you outside."

Five minutes later, they were on their way. Crescent View didn't sport a whole lot of retail shopping experiences—at least not yet—but it did have some of the best parks and picnic areas in the region. Just about anywhere you went you could find a small lake, a field of wildflowers and a gravel walkway.

One of the nicest, Bluebonnet Park, was right behind Carried Away's shopping center. After stopping at the café to grab two bottles of iced tea, they took the path to the park, Minnie keeping an eye on Wanda to make sure she didn't get overheated.

Not too many people were at the park. Probably had something to do with the ninety-degree day. In no time at all, they were sitting on a wooden bench under a bright yellow canvas tarp.

After a fortifying sip of tea, Wanda said, "First things first. What did Peter have to say?"

"All kinds of things. He's miserable in Dallas, couldn't find any women there to give him the time of day and has now decided that I'm better than nothing."

"I never did like him, Minnie."

"I know." Across the way, a mom was pushing a trio of toddlers on the swing set, walking up and down nonstop as the little girls squealed their delight. Minnie smiled, wondering who was going to be the most ready for an afternoon nap.

"Anyway, right after I told Peter that I've moved on, he spies Matt Madigan across the way, drinking coffee and minding his own business, then starts up saying how a guy like that would never want anything to do with someone like me."

"*Like you?* What does that mean?"

"You know. Peter knows I'm not pretty or thin enough for a guy like Matt."

"He's wrong, dear. I hope you told him to keep his unwanted opinions to himself."

"I didn't have to, because Matt overheard. Next thing I know, Matt's pretending that we have something going on, tells Peter goodbye, and then gives me the kind of kiss that curls toes." Realizing that was probably an inappropriate detail, she murmured, "Sorry, Wanda."

But her neighbor only sipped her tea and smiled. "I may be old but I've been toe-curling kissed a time or two myself." Wanda fanned herself dramatically. "I always knew you and Matt were going to work out your differences."

"We didn't. Matt and I are still business enemies."

"Do we have to stew on this again?"

"No. It doesn't matter, anyway. I talked to Brenda and Abel just an hour ago and we have a plan. We're going to join forces along with some other business owners and come up with a sign campaign to fight SavNGo."

"A sign campaign?"

"Yes. Brenda has already taken the order to the printing store. We're going to post Support Our Stores signs all over Crescent View. SOS, for short. Just to remind people that there are business people who're trying to make a living right here, right now."

"I hope it works." Wanda chuckled as all three toddlers started crying across the way and the mom started putting them in the red wagon to take them home. "Oh, I remember those days. Kids crying and the day not even half-over." Looking over at Minnie, Wanda said, "You and Matthew are two of the finest people I know. It would be a shame to not try and iron out your differences."

"I do like him, Wanda. I liked kissing him just fine. And I love that he and Kimber get along so well. But attraction can only take a relationship so far."

"Work isn't everything."

"But it's all I've got right now. I can't forget my responsibilities."

"Minnie Clark, is Matt the one who's making you feel that you have to choose between him and your store…or is it you?"

"Me," she whispered. "But somehow that doesn't make things any easier."

TWO EVENINGS LATER, after work, after dinner of hot dogs and Tater Tots, after a long bubble bath, Kimber made a pronouncement.

"I don't want to be a Kimber no more."

"Anymore," Minnie corrected absently as she combed out a part in Kimber's wet curly hair. Then, as the words sank in, she said, "If you don't want to be a Kimber, who do you want to be?"

"Princess Kaitlin Dream Princess."

"My word! I never heard of a name with two princesses in it. That's pretty special." Minnie wanted to jump up and down. Finally her difficult, sad niece was behaving more like the little girl she was.

"Princess Kaitlin Dream Princess only wears purple."

"Thank goodness you've got on a purple nightgown."

Kimber nodded importantly. "Purple's special."

Quickly Minnie braided Kimber's hair, happy to play along. "Maybe we could make you a crown, Your Highness." Minnie and Paige had spent hours pretending to be princesses and horses and race car drivers. Anything but sisters living in a little Texas town.

But instead of erupting in giggles, Kimber only nodded. "I'm gonna need a crown because Princess Kaitlin Dream Princess is really special. More special than being plain ol' Kimber."

Minnie's hand stilled as she tied off the braid. Maybe this wasn't about pretending, after all.

Maybe there was something going on here. "I like Kimber. I don't think the name or the girl is plain at all."

"I just wanna be special."

Hair done, Minnie shifted and knelt in front of her niece. "You already are."

"Do you think Mommy thought so?"

Oh, what had brought that on? Treading carefully, Minnie said, "I know she did. Every time we talked, she talked about how special you were."

"Every time?"

"Every time. I promise."

With a heavy sigh, Kimber turned and looked at herself in the mirror. Catching Minnie's eye, she said, "I wish Mommy wasn't up in heaven."

"Me, too."

"I miss her."

"I do, too. And I know something else. I know your mommy and daddy didn't want to leave you. They loved you. Just like I love you, too."

"I hope nothing happens to you."

"Nothing will. We're going to be together for a long time."

Brown eyes, duplicates of Paige's, widened. "Promise?"

"I promise." Minnie hoped nothing ever happened to break that promise.

"Can I still be Princess Kaitlin Dream Princess?"

"Sure, but I think I'm just going to have to call you Kimber. I can't remember all those names."

Kimber bit her lip. "I'm not going to call you Mommy."

"That's okay. We can stick to my name, too. I'll call you Kimber and you call me Minnie."

"Can I still make a crown?"

Minnie glanced at her watch. "If we can make one in twenty minutes before bedtime. Go get the construction paper, honey. I'll find the scissors and tape."

As Kimber marched off, Minnie braced a shaking hand on the counter. Could it be that the two of them had finally reached a new place?

Minnie hoped that was true.

Chapter Thirteen

From the moment Jackie Vance showed up in Crescent View, gossips started talking. Matt figured it had something to do with Jackie's inky-black hair sliding along her shoulders, mingling with the silkiness of the sleek scarves she favored. Maybe it had to do with Jackie's penchant for designer heels. Matt, for one, had never seen Jackie in flats.

He'd never seen her in anything but expensive, stylish suits, either.

And though he'd told her Crescent View was more of a Kool-Aid and burger kind of place than martinis and sushi, Jackie had arrived in town looking ready for the Next Big Thing.

Which, actually, was her.

With the type of searching that would make a bloodhound proud, Lane located Jackie within thirty minutes of her arrival.

After knocking on the door at Mrs. Wy's, he let himself in and stationed himself near the stairs, just to catch sight of her.

And then he looked as lovestruck as an elk in mating season. The whole situation was unnerving. Lane had been pretty tough to deal with ever since Matt had had to ask him to rebid. Now, though, he was acting as if they were back in high school and best buds again. Matt didn't know whether to slug the guy or just be relieved that finally he was going to be forgiven.

Reluctantly, Matt performed the introductions. "Jackie, this is Lane. Lane, Jackie."

Lane puffed up like he'd just received a burst of hot air. "Hi. I own Henderson HVAC." With a sideways glance at Matt, he added, "My company's currently re-bidding for the heating and electrical for Crescent View's SavNGo."

To Matt's amusement, Jackie played it cool. "I know who you are."

"How?"

"I'm Matt's assistant. We've been working together on the bids."

"Oh."

Though Jackie was staring at her nails, complete with shiny white tips, Matt had the curious feeling that she was focused on Lane all the way. "Matt's mentioned you, too. Ya'll went to school together, right?"

"Right. We played ball together for years."

Up went one finely arched eyebrow. "Ball?"

Pushing back his cap, Lane grinned. "Football."

Jackie had the nerve to look intrigued. "Matt, I didn't know you ever played football."

Matt knew she'd never cared. They didn't talk personal histories; they discussed timetables and contracts. "Jackie, what the heck?"

"Sorry, Matt. I'll behave."

Lane grinned as he walked beside Jackie, following Matt into the kitchen. "Please don't."

Matt was tempted to run the faucet cold, then splash them both with a bucket of icy water. "Want to have a seat?"

Jackie posed, one hip out. Just like some girl on *America's Next Top Model*. "I'm fine."

Lane stepped closer. "Yes, you are."

Matt tried not to throw up as fireworks kept going off between the two of them.

"Settle down, ya'll," Matt murmured.

Both ignored him. Lane was actually looking kind of starstruck. "How long are you here for?"

"One week. Maybe two."

Lane's green eyes settled on Jackie's form in a way that made Matt want to give them some space, quickly. "That's hardly long enough to get used to this Texas heat."

"I'm not here to get hot. Just work. I've been Matt's assistant for years. We have a hard time getting anything done on the phone."

Lane slid a you-sly-dog look his way. Matt batted it to one side. "Jackie and I are co-workers."

Lane jumped in with both feet. "There's not anything between you two?"

"No," Matt said. "Not ever."

Jackie leaned Lane's way. "Why?"

Lane started talking before Matt could run interference. He'd always been too dumb for his own good. "Well, you are just about the prettiest thing I've seen in ages, that's why."

Matt scowled. Jackie did not need any of these tired good ol' boy advances. "Shut up, Lane."

Lane didn't. "Are you seeing anyone?"

"Are you asking?" Interest sparking in her eyes, Jackie ran her hands down the seam of her skirt.

Lane followed the motion.

"Hold on, now. Maybe you two could do this some-where else? Away from me?"

They kept talking as if he wasn't there. "I am."

"I was seeing someone, but it didn't work out. So I'm definitely single."

"Do you have plans tonight? Can I take you to dinner?"

Matt shook his head. "Actually—"

Jackie interrupted. "Yes."

"I'll pick you up at seven," Lane said, right before he picked up the keys he'd tossed onto the counter and strode out the back door.

After Lane left, Matt turned to Jackie, who had made a mini-transformation. Gone was the sexy siren. In her place was the woman he'd come to depend on. No longer posing, she was sitting primly on one of the kitchen chairs, glasses on, and thumbing through files. She could have been in a cubicle at the office.

"What the hell was that all about?"

Jackie batted her eyes. "That's called getting asked out on a date. You ought to try it sometime, Matt."

"But you're here to work."

"I know. And I will work. But even you and I can't work all the time." She opened up her laptop like they hadn't just been playing the dating game, right there at Mrs. Wy's dining room table. "Ready to finalize those reports?"

"No. Aren't we going to talk about this? I don't want Lane to hurt you. He's under the impression he's a ladies' man."

"I think I can handle him. Besides, it's just dinner, Matt. Don't worry." She pushed her notes to him. "Now, I was thinking we might need to rethink section K in this report. It doesn't read right."

Matt got sucked in, in spite of himself. For an hour, they went over facts and figures and words and expenses. Everything moved like clockwork when she was there.

Strangely enough, it was Jackie who broke concentration. "Can you believe he thought there was something cooking between you and me?"

"I can believe it. We are about the same age and single. People talk."

She chuckled. "I'm just sitting here, thinking about kissing you. It would be so weird."

Curious, Matt looked at her lips and tried to imagine getting up close and personal with them. Nope. Even the thought of it was laughable.

Though Jackie was attractive, she wasn't his type. He preferred a more gentle type of gal, a woman who needed him. He'd spent too many days and nights feeling out of place. The last thing he wanted was a Jackie-style lady. A lady where the simplest conversation could turn into a battle of wills. "We'd be horrible together. I can't even imagine kissing you. No offense."

"None taken."

But masculine vanity did kick in. "You know, I've had women tell me that I'm damned attractive."

Jackie tilted her head. "Attractive men are a dime a dozen, Matt. A good boss like you? That's what's priceless. Besides, I could never get past those blue eyes of yours."

"What's wrong with my eyes?"

"They're too blue."

"I sure hope Lane knows what he's getting into."

"He will." Checking her watch, she pointed to his cell

phone. "Better get on your cell. We've got the VP in five minutes. Ready to give him the update?"

"As ready as I'll ever be."

Chapter Fourteen

"Thank God you answered," Minnie said in a rush the minute Matt picked up his phone.

"Minnie? You okay?"

"I'm fine. But Matt—it's Wanda."

Matt put down his pen. In the two days since Jackie had arrived, Matt had hardly seen Minnie. Actually, they'd been so busy, he and his assistant had hardly talked with anyone who didn't either work for SavNGo or have a new bid in for Store 35.

"Mrs. Wy?"

"Matt, she just got taken to North Texas Hospital."

With the flick of a switch, concern for Minnie was replaced by pure shock. Mrs. Wy was a rock in his life. He'd never contemplated her getting really sick. "What happened?"

To his right, Jackie looked up from her laptop. Her fingers stilled and concern etched her features. For once, she pushed her work aside and listened in.

"I'm not sure," Minnie said. "Wanda called me in a panic, and I ran right over. She was in her kitchen, pale as a ghost. I immediately called 9-1-1." Minnie paused. "She looks bad, Matt. The EMTs said it might be her heart. But one thought it might be heat stroke or maybe something to do with her kidneys," she added in a rush. "I'm really worried. Her skin looked gray when the paramedics came and she didn't seem to know what was going on."

"Where are you now?"

"Standing in your front yard. The ambulance just left. Your house is still unlocked. What…what do you need me to do?"

"Sit tight. I'll be right there."

"You sure?"

"Positive." With a hurried look at Jackie, he said, "Jackie's here with me. She can stay here and hold down the fort." When Jackie gave him a thumbs-up sign, he reached for his keys. "I'm ten minutes away. I'll come pick you up."

"I can meet you—"

Minnie sounded so shaken up, there was no way he wanted her to drive. Truth be told, he wasn't in too good shape, either. If something happened to Mrs. Wy, Matt privately didn't know if he could handle it. "I'm on my way. You can fill me in on what you know while we drive. I'll be there as soon as I can."

"Okay. Thanks, Matt."

Jackie twirled a pencil in between her fingers. "Wanda's sick?"

"An ambulance just picked her up. I'm going to get Minnie and head over to the hospital." Worriedly, he looked at their mess of a work area. They'd spent the day shuffling moneys, doing their best to appease the local workers and the powers-that-be up in Philly. "Do you want to continue this or take a break?"

"I'll make more phone calls and get that report done.

You go. Tell Wanda I hope she feels better." A frown marred her features. "She's such a nice lady."

"She is at that. I'll let Lane know you're here."

"You do that." She smiled wickedly. "Matter of fact, tell Lane I'm all alone." Waving a hand, she pushed him on his way. "Now, go on, Matt."

He didn't need any more urging. Grabbing his sunglasses, he hustled to his truck, fielding a couple of questions from the work crew as he ran. As soon as everyone heard Wanda's name, offers came fast and furious to help.

Easing right back into small-town life, Matt passed on what he knew and promised he'd relay any information about Wanda.

After racing through the town square, past the old train station, and the closed five-and-dime, Matt directed his truck to the twin white water towers and finally pulled onto his street ten minutes later.

He was startled by the sight of Kimber sitting on Minnie's lap on her front steps when he pulled up in front of the house. He just assumed she'd be in school, then he remembered that one of his workers had mentioned that it was a teacher's in-service day.

Worry lines marred Kimber's brow as she, too, looked up at Matt in alarm. Carefully he schooled his expression. It wouldn't help anyone if he increased their panic. "Can I offer you girls a lift?"

"Matt!" Kimber cried out, clambering away from Minnie and scrambling over to his truck. "We've got to go to the hospital!"

"I heard." Crossing in front of his truck, he leaned down and swung all fifty pounds of girl into his arms. He glanced toward Minnie, who approached them at a

far slower pace. As she neared, Matt noticed that her eyes were misty. Obviously she'd been trying her best to hold everything in. "You ready?"

"I am." Her face cleared with relief. "Thanks."

Holding Kimber's tote full of coloring books and toys, Minnie climbed into the cab. After buckling Kimber up in the backseat, she met his gaze.

Matt's heart skidded a bit. He liked the feeling of being needed. Of her finding solace in his presence. "It's going to be okay," he said.

"I hope so," she murmured as he pulled away from the curb. Matt was so aware of her. He *felt* her presence. Caught the scent of cherry and vanilla again.

And experienced that same sense of loss about what could have been. Did Minnie ever wonder if the two of them would one day be able to get over the hurdle of Store 35 and be together?

Almost immediately, shame slammed him hard in the gut. Wanda was sitting in the hospital. There were other things to think about. A whole lot of other things.

THERE WERE TOO MANY machines and not enough Mrs. Wyzecki to go around. That was the immediate impression Matt got from the first minute he stepped into her room. Minnie was staying back in the waiting room since Kimber couldn't enter the ICU. They'd heard from the hospital staff that a few more people from the community were already on their way over, too, so soon Minnie would have all the help she needed to watch Kimber if she wanted to visit Mrs. Wy as well.

Luckily his foster mom was conscious and alert. Alert enough for her to fasten her sharp eyes on him when he entered. "Matthew."

He matched her snippy tone. "Mrs. Wy. I don't like this. Not one bit."

Mrs. Wy smiled wanly, her fierce expression doing more to show her spunk than her tiny body, lying prone and at the machines' mercy. "I don't recall asking you what you wanted."

He crossed to her and gently took her hand. "How you doing?"

"About as well as can be expected for someone with a brand-new heart problem."

"Brand-new?"

She looked away guiltily. "New enough."

"I'm beginning to have an idea that maybe this isn't so new." Matt had found out from the doctor on call that Mrs. Wy had already been diagnosed with heart disease. "I don't recall you mentioning one word about heart disease when we were eating steaks and peach cobbler the other evening."

Showing the same amount of gumption that had gotten Matt and a whole series of foster children in line, she waved a hand to stop his lecture.

Just like all those years ago, he abruptly halted his tirade. "Ma'am?"

"Hush now. I'm seventy-four, Matthew."

"Seventy-four isn't old anymore."

"You could have fooled this heart."

"Well, you're just going to have to get better. I need you around a whole lot longer. I'm going to take care of you from here on out, you hear me?"

"I hear you." With a frown, she said, "I hope they remove some of these tubes soon. They're going to pump me so full of fluids I fear I'm going to float away."

"You just need to concentrate on getting better. And

behave when they wheel you around for tests. I'm worried about you."

"Don't talk to me like a child."

"Don't be here again and I won't."

She shifted positions. Matt hurried to adjust the pillow beneath her head. "While I'm in here, you've got things to do."

"Such as?"

"Your job. People around here are depending on that SavNGo to go up in a timely manner, Matthew."

He shook his head. "I've got plenty of bosses. Jackie's here, too. I don't need you telling me what to do, too."

"My advice is free. Listen, I also want you to work on my house. You're gonna be able to get a lot done without me underfoot."

He hated the idea of being in her home without her, never mind putting the emptiness to good use. "Only you would say something like that."

"It's true. Now you can forge full steam ahead."

She was talking as though she planned to stay at the hospital for a while. "How long are you planning to be here? What did the doctors say?"

For the first time, her expression mirrored her frail condition. "Not too much. They seem to be real fond of keeping secrets."

"That's not right. I'll get to the bottom of things."

"I'll look forward to it."

A brief knock interrupted their conversation. After introductions, Matt said, "Dr. Garcia, what's going on?"

"Wanda's been going too strong. She needs to take things a little bit easier."

"And?"

Dr. Garcia glanced at Mrs. Wy. "Perhaps we could speak in the hall?"

As ornery as ever, Mrs. Wy shook her head. "I don't think so."

Matt was losing his patience. "Mrs. Wy—"

"Matthew, Doctor, I stopped being treated like a baby when my little sister was born, some seventy years ago. What is my prognosis?"

To Matt's surprise, Dr. Garcia carefully came over and took Mrs. Wy's hand. "The truth is you've got some blockage in your arteries. Your prescribed exercise and diet regime don't seem to have helped much."

Matt held up a hand. "Hold on, here. Mrs. Wy, *prescribed exercise and diet?*"

"Hush, Matthew. Doctor, what do we need to do?"

"We're going to keep you here longer than you're going to want to be and run some more tests. Wanda, I think you might have had a mild heart attack." He took a deep breath, then turned to Matt. "If the test results come back the way I think they will, we're going to have to do some surgery."

This was Matt's worst nightmare. "When?"

"Probably within the next day or so."

Mrs. Wy paled. "Heart surgery?"

"I'm hoping for an angioplasty. That's minimally invasive. With any luck, you'll be out of here within the week. Then you're going to have to start taking my words seriously, young lady."

"Raymond Garcia, you watch your mouth." There was enough spice and vinegar in her voice to toss a salad.

"I'll watch my mouth when you start listening, Wanda." The doctor's lips twitched. "You don't suffer fools, do you?"

"Not in seventy-four years."

"We're going to talk about some things, she and I," Matt said.

"Maybe we should." Wearily, she sighed. "You know, come to think of it, I'm feeling kind of tired."

"This is the best place for you," Dr. Garcia said. "I'll make sure you get the best care that we can provide." He squeezed her hand. "Now try to rest."

Matt left the room when a nurse joined the doctor and they took more blood and Dr. Garcia spoke to Mrs. Wy on his own. He was still holding up the wall when the other man joined him outside. "Any questions, Matt?"

"Not at the moment." He held out a hand. "Thanks. I know bending Wanda's ear isn't an easy thing to do. She's conned me into doing more things I didn't want to over the years than I can count."

"I'd say her knack is alive and well." Raymond Garcia chuckled as he glanced at Wanda's closed door. "I usually don't act so unprofessionally. I have to tell you, seeing her getting wheeled in here on a gurney hit me hard. I've known Mrs. Wyzecki for a long time. She was a best friend's foster mother."

"She took me in, too. I owe her a lot."

"We're going to do everything we can for her here."

"And I'll make sure she takes better care of herself in the future," Matt promised.

"I'll hold you to it."

"Matthew?" Mrs. Wyzecki's voice might have been frail, but it still packed a punch, even through the closed door.

"I guess I'm getting paged." Matt hurried in. "Mrs. Wy, you're supposed to be resting."

"Kind of hard to do that with you young men yakking in the hall."

"Did you need something?"

"Yes. If what Dr. Garcia says is true, I won't be going to the condo anytime soon. I'll have to go someplace a little different." She swallowed hard. "Start looking into assisted-care centers, would you?"

"No, ma'am, I will not. You can come back to your own home." The idea taking root, he grabbed hold of it, tight. "We can live together."

Though she shook her head no, Matt was pretty sure he'd spied a spark of interest in her eyes. He rushed on before she could say a word. "We've done just fine so far. And it is your home, after all."

"You're too young to have an old lady roommate."

"No...I don't think so. Actually, I kind of like the idea. Think about it, will you, Mrs. Wyzecki?"

"I'll think about it. Maybe it would work for a little while." She met his gaze. "And Matthew, don't you think it's time you started calling me Wanda? Roommates call each other by their first names, you know."

He swallowed the lump that had just formed in his throat. "All right. Wanda, I'm glad we're going to be living together for a bit longer."

"Good. Now get on with you. I'm gonna take a nap before somebody gets a bug in their ear and decides they need to take more of my blood." After a pause she whispered. "It's going to take some work to make the house a home for us two, you know."

Matt grinned, now that he knew he'd won. "We'll do it together, Wanda."

A faint smile bloomed before fading into slumber. "That's what I like to hear. Go on, now."

Chapter Fifteen

The moment Minnie spied Matt pulling into his driveway later that afternoon, she grabbed Kimber's hand and led her across the street. They found him standing in the middle of about a hundred boxes in the garage.

Matt looked as worn-out as an old dishrag. Seeing the weariness in his gaze made her want to push her own worries and problems to one side.

Especially since the look he gave Kimber brightened the girl's day. "Kimber, look at you. I like those shoes."

Kimber was wearing black patent Mary Janes along with a bumble bee-bright skirt and a white T-shirt. She'd been twirling around all afternoon, making the skirt puff up. "Me, too. Minnie says they're *fancy* shoes."

"They are, at that."

Kimber scampered closer. "Whatcha doin?"

"Sitting here, trying to figure out what to do with all these boxes."

Kimber spun around. "Oh. You coming inside?"

Matt glanced Minnie's way. "Sooner or later."

Kimber spun again on one foot, then came to a stop with a big sigh. "Matt, all this dancing is making me thirsty. Real thirsty."

"You hot?"

"Uh-huh." Kimber wiped her brow dramatically. "It's hot as July."

That was a Wanda Wyzecki expression if he'd ever heard one. Matt's lips twitched. "The air's on. Want to go check on Mrs. Wy's kitty and fish?"

"Yep."

She skipped on her way inside. Minnie approached much more slowly. They'd had so many awkward conversations over the past few months that she wasn't sure anymore how to say simple things—like she hoped he was okay. "How is Wanda?" There had been so many well-wishers coming to see Wanda, Minnie and Kimber had gone home to avoid overwhelming the older lady.

"Not good." He kicked one of the boxes. Not hard, just enough to give it a good nudge. "It turns out she's been fighting high cholesterol for some time. Well, she's been fighting it half-heartedly."

"She's so slim, I had no idea."

"Neither did I." With a frown, he added, "After you left, the doctor said she's going to need surgery. An angioplasty or something."

"Oh, my."

Just the thought of Wanda being on the operating table gave him the shakes. "The doc said the procedure wasn't too invasive, and that she should get through it just fine, but…"

Minnie finished the thought for him. "It's still her heart. And it's still scary."

"Exactly. She's always been so tough, so spunky and vibrant. I don't want to think of her in any other way."

"So when are they going to decide whether or not she needs this done?"

"They're going to do one more test, but between you and me, Dr. Garcia sounded pretty certain. And he doesn't seem like the kind of guy who throws around words like 'heart disease' willy-nilly."

"Matt Madigan, you have to be the first man I've ever met who says willy-nilly."

As she'd hoped, he chuckled. "It's from hanging out in this house. I'm starting to adopt all her strange little habits."

"If you start watering pansies in a housecoat, I'll get worried."

"If I ever even know what a housecoat is, I'm going to get worried!"

"Kimber and I came over to see if you needed any help. Do you want me to make you some dinner or clean up a bit? I can do laundry if you'd like."

"I can do laundry, Min. There's plenty of food, too." With a worried look around the garage, he said, "I've just got to figure out what to do with all this stuff." Grabbing an antique brass clock, he murmured, "Plans have changed. I think Wanda and I are going to live together."

"I like that idea."

"Yeah?"

"Definitely." Minnie wasn't as surprised by the news as she would've thought she would be. Privately, she thought Matt needed Wanda just as much as she needed him.

Actually the four of them—Wanda, Matt, Kimber and herself were a sure set of mismatched souls.

"Anyway, I told her I'd try my best to put everything in order as best I can. Wanda pretty much said she'd kick my butt if I didn't."

Minnie wondered where his partner was. "Where's Jackie?"

Matt grimaced. "That's a whole other source of aggravation. Jackie came here to help dig me out of all my paperwork, but she's not working all that much. At the moment, she's out with Lane. Again."

That made Minnie smile. Just the other day Lane and Jackie had run into her store and visited for a bit. There'd been so much heat between them that Minnie had been tempted to turn on the fans. "I guess they've really hit it off. You're not jealous, are you?"

"I'm not jealous at all. Jackie's like a really irritating, know-it-all sister. It's the whole situation that I'm finding disturbing. See, I'd been under the impression Lane would set his sights on a small-town girl. And Jackie's supposed to be only thinking about work. But the two of them are acting like there's something serious going on." With a look of confusion, Matt turned to her. "Min, how do people fall in love so fast?"

She shrugged. "Some just do, I guess." What else could she say? Though Matt would be the last person to broadcast it, she knew losing both parents young had made him antsy about trusting and relationships.

She could say the same for herself. After all, she'd thought she'd done everything right for Peter and had gotten pushed aside the moment things started turning out different than planned.

Minnie thought Matt looked adorable. Once again, she couldn't fight the attraction that always was front and center whenever he was nearby. Before she could mind her words better, she murmured, "You know, sometimes temptation can't be helped."

Matt's cheeks stained red as he glanced in her direction, then looked quickly away. "I realize that."

Suddenly it was too hot in that garage. Had she ever

felt so keyed up and tingly around Peter? He'd been attractive. She'd known he'd been anxious to take her to bed. But for some reason, she'd never felt the same. Something had been missing between them. Something tender and compelling.

Eager to break the tension, Minnie walked toward a box. "You know what? Things will go quicker if I help you seal some of these. Hand me the packing tape, would you?"

As soon as he handed it over, Minnie got to work. With even motions, she taped and tore, labeling the boxes while Matt stacked them in some sign of order. A line of sweat formed in the middle of his back, creating a dark patch in the midst of bleached white. Minnie felt moisture dampen between her breasts and on her brow. She hastily pulled a rubber band from her pocket and fastened her hair into a high ponytail.

"I like it like that," he said out of nowhere.

"My hair up?" Honestly, Minnie hadn't known he ever thought about her hair. "It gets hot. I should probably cut it all off."

He scowled. "I sure as hell hope you don't."

"Uh, what?"

"I mean…I've always liked your hair. It's pretty."

"Thanks." All kinds of compliments for Matt rattled around her brain, daring Minnie to utter them. About how she loved his eyes. How she appreciated the way he looked in those worn Wranglers. How he always made her feel just the right size instead of two sizes too big. "Matt, I've always thought you…"

"I what?"

"Were good-looking." Oh, great. How lame could she be?

Matt straightened. "Really?"

"Minnie, come quick!"

All thoughts of clumsy flirting dissipated when Minnie saw Kimber's face. Thick tears were rolling down her cheeks. "Honey? Are you hurt?"

"No." She hiccupped. "I've been playing with Mrs. Wy's kitty. But when I looked in the fish tank, one was floating on top. It died!"

Minnie wrapped her arms around her niece. Kimber was in such a fragile position that nearly about anything unforeseen was a recipe for disaster. The family counselor had told Minnie to not overreact or discount those feelings. "Oh, honey. I'm sorry."

Uh-oh, Matt mouthed to Minnie. Out loud, he said, "I guess we'd better go see. You said it was floating? By its lonesome?"

Kimber nodded, reaching for his hand as they walked in. "It doesn't want to swim no more. What happened?"

Matt shrugged, again looking Minnie's way. She motioned to him with a hand. It was almost a relief to see that someone else didn't have a handle on knowing the right thing to say, either.

Minnie hid a smile as he answered, as calm and sober as a minister on Sunday. "Fish don't last very long. I guess it was its time to go to fish heaven."

The three of them made a semicircle around the tank and dutifully looked in. Sure enough, there was a goldfish listlessly floating on its side. "It's dead, all right," Kimber pronounced.

"I'm sure it had a good life," Minnie said.

Matt nodded. "I, for one, liked living here. I bet Mr. Orange Fish did, too."

"Is that its name?"

It was almost comical, the expression that came over Matt's face. "I don't believe it had a name. I just made that up."

"I liked Mr. Orange Fish," Kimber said. "Will Mrs. Wy be mad?"

"I don't think so. I seem to recall this happening before." He dropped Kimber's hand. "Well, I'll get out the net and take care of things."

Kimber nodded solemnly, looking like a mini-princess in her black-and-yellow outfit. "And I'll look for a box."

Matt froze. "You want to bury it?"

"Uh-huh. Can we?"

"Go find a box in the pantry, honey," Matt said. "I think I spied some little cereal boxes like I used to get on the airplane. One of those should do just fine."

"I'll line it all with tissue."

"Good idea. You make it comfortable, then we'll bury this little guy proper."

When they were alone, Minnie whispered, "You're pretty amazing. Most guys would've pushed her feelings aside."

"I hope not. I have a feeling that funerals are pretty important to her right now."

"I imagine they are." Looking down the hall, Minnie hoped Kimber was going to be able to handle things okay. They'd come so far; she couldn't bear it if this whole episode set her back.

His cell rang. Matt looked at the display, then said reluctantly, "I've got to take this. It's work."

Minnie used the time to check out the pantry with Kimber.

"Do you think Corn Pops or Rice Krispies?"

"I like the blue box. I think the fish will like it, too."

Carefully they prepared the box, slipping a bunch of folded tissues inside. As best she could, Minnie plopped the fish in the middle, then proceeded to close up the whole thing.

To her surprise, Kimber looked pleased with how the funeral arrangements were going. She directed Minnie on how to tape the box shut, and then decided the box needed a tray to rest on while they were waiting for burial.

When Matt got off the phone, the three of them marched outside. "There's a lot of woods back here. Look good to you?"

Kimber shook her head. "Animals will get him. I want him here, near the pool."

Matt readily agreed. They wound back around the pool, weaving in between the thicket of pine trees and overgrown shrubs. Finally Kimber picked a place near the diving board, right under a blooming rosebush.

"This spot does look just right," Matt said, then knelt down on one knee and dug a little hole. Without ceremony, Minnie placed Mr. Orange Fish into his eternal resting place.

Just as Matt picked up a pile of dirt and was about to toss it in the hole. Kimber tugged on his sleeve. "Wait!" she cried. "We're not done. Minnie, you've gotta say a prayer."

Minnie realized that it did seem strange not to say anything at all. "Dear Lord, please let Mr. Orange Fish rest in peace." She sneaked a peek at Kimber, whose eyes were scrunched up so tightly she looked about to give herself a doozy of a headache.

To her surprise, Matt reached out a hand and took Kimber's little one. "He was a good fish," he added.

Kimber nodded. "Lord, please don't let Mrs. Wyzecki miss this fish too much. Make sure she knows that he's up in heaven with his other friends, probably swimming in a bright blue ocean. And please look after everyone up in heaven. Like Mommy and Daddy. Amen."

"Amen," Minnie and Matt repeated.

"That was a good service," Matt said as he covered up the box with dirt.

Like a little soldier, Kimber stood by, watching him, her lip quivering with unspent emotion. Minnie knelt down and opened her arms.

After a first hesitant step, Kimber rushed forward, flinging her arms around Minnie's neck, holding on tight. "Do you think he's okay now?"

"I know he is. You were right about the funeral. This was the perfect thing to do."

After another moment, Matt cleared his throat. "Are y'all ready to go in?" He pointed to the sky. "A storm's coming."

Sure enough, the clouds were gray and ominous. Minnie knew those clouds. Within seconds, a torrential downpour could occur and they'd get drenched. "I think so," she said softly, running her hand through Kimber's long mass of curls and feeling that a breakthrough had just come about.

She didn't need to be a grief counselor to know that Kimber had needed some control over a funeral. Thinking back to the funerals in Arizona, Minnie recalled that all of them were so dazed that no one had thought much about Kimber's wishes. All they'd counted on was getting things done as best as possible without dissolving into inconsolable grief.

But today, with Matt's help, they'd reached another turning point.

They ran into the house just as the first thick raindrops fell, and Minnie thought that maybe she and Matt were going to be okay, too. Her immature infatuation had turned into something far brighter and more meaningful. She now didn't put him on a pedestal, hoping to one day be good enough, popular enough, pretty enough to climb up there with him.

Now she saw him as a man. He had his own insecurities and needs, as she did.

Even if they never became more than what they were, Minnie supposed she would still appreciate his friendship. Life had taught her that friends were as hard to come by as good boyfriends.

While the rain pounded the windows, Matt turned to them. "Want to stay for dinner?"

"Sure." She wasn't ready to go home just yet.

"Good." His face didn't betray his emotions or give her a hint of what he was thinking.

But she didn't care. For once, she wanted to be completely selfish and live in the moment. She liked being with Matt. He made her feel good.

And that was enough.

Chapter Sixteen

"What do you girls think about chicken and potatoes? Mrs. Wy has some frozen casseroles in the freezer."

Minnie looked at Kimber. "Chicken sounds fine with me. What about you?"

"I like chicken."

Matt couldn't resist smiling. The little girl had been in a whirlwind of emotion that evening, but finally had settled down. Well, until she jumped up again. "Oh, no! George is home alone!"

Before she launched into another mini-drama, Matt held out a hand. "Let's grab an umbrella and go get him."

"I'll get the dinner started," Minnie said, giving him a grateful look.

Matt saw new lines of worry around her eyes. Kimber wasn't the only one who seemed emotionally drained.

"You ready to run in the storm?"

"I'm ready!"

He clutched her hand and ran into the weather, bullets of raindrops beating the nylon over their heads and puddles of water bathing their feet. Matt stood at the door while Kimber got George's cage, then locked Minnie's door and escorted them back.

"Thanks, Matt," she whispered.

"You're welcome." In no time, Kimber had spread out an old quilt of Wanda's and was sitting with her pet in front of the TV. George seemed to be the only guinea pig on the face of the earth that enjoyed being cuddled. Kimber was speaking to him in soft tones and gently petting him. George replied by squeaking nonstop.

Pleased to see Kimber happy, Matt joined Minnie in the kitchen. "I suppose she's got a lot to tell George."

Minnie glanced over at her niece. "Today's been pretty incredible. My mom's going to smile when she hears about the fish funeral."

"I've noticed I've been smiling a lot, too, in spite of how sad the whole thing was. Poor kid. Mrs. Wy's going to be sorry she missed the big event."

"Or sorry that it ever happened."

"I don't know about that," he said, pretty much reading her mind. "I think Kimber needed that activity, even though it was at the expense of the fish."

"Thanks for not minding about the funeral."

"I care about her, too, Min. I understand." Needing something to do, he picked out a bottle of cabernet from Mrs. Wy's wine rack. "Glass of wine?"

"Thanks."

After pouring two glasses, he said, "You're doing a good job with Kimber, Minnie."

"You think so? Every day brings a new challenge. Sometimes I feel we're going three steps back to go one forward."

"Lately, I've been feeling the same way. But, the thing about that girl is that she's got a good heart."

"Thanks for saying that, but I think we both know I can't take any credit for her goodness. She and Jeremy and Paige are responsible for that." After taking a fortifying sip of her wine, she murmured, "Taking care of her has been one of the hardest things I've ever done. And, once more, I don't know if I'm ever going to get good at it."

"You will. Family is what counts. You'll do it for Paige."

His words, and the fierce longing in them, made her want to open up a little bit more. Encouraged Minnie to confide things she was afraid to confess to anyone.

Oh, shoot. She might as well say it. "I'm not sure why Paige wanted me to have Kimber."

Thinking of the animosity she and her sister had shared over the years, Minnie whispered, "Sometimes I think she made a big mistake."

Just like with Kimber, Matt took her words to heart and thought about them carefully before replying. "I don't think so. I can't imagine Paige ever thought about not being around to see Kimber grow up. But she must have known something for sure—that you'd love your niece like she was your own."

To Minnie's surprise, she realized that was true. No matter how difficult the transition had been from single shop owner to full-time adoptive mom, she'd never wavered in her intention to be the best mother she could possibly be to Kimber.

However, all the love in the world couldn't solve her problems. Or make the things she'd done wrong better. "But—"

"Take it from someone who would've given a lot of money for a healthy dose of unconditional love. Love counts. It counts a lot."

"Didn't your dad love you?"

Matt thought about all the times his father hadn't

been around for him. The times when he'd been so distant they might as well have been living in separate states. But admitting that seemed too weak. "He did when I won a game."

Minnie didn't meet his halfhearted smile. Instead, pure compassion and understanding filled her gaze. "And other times?"

"And other times, he wasn't around much." Matt picked up a piece of wilted lettuce and tossed it in the sink. "I loved him, and I know he loved me. But…in some ways he was gone way before he died. In some ways, he left the moment my mom died."

"Wanda has mentioned that things weren't as easy for you as most people thought. You fooled a lot of people, Matt. I, for one, thought you had everything."

"I had a good arm. I had a cocky attitude." He chuckled. "Back then, I tried to make that be enough. And when we had a homecoming parade, or a pep rally, or a college scout came by and people said my name, it felt like it was almost enough. But when I'd go home no one would be there. The place would be so empty. And the rooms would feel like I did on the inside. Cold and alone."

Her heart went out to him. Even though things hadn't been perfect in her house—she'd grown up in Paige's shadow—she'd always known she'd belonged. "Wanda loved you."

He chuckled. "She did. She was the first person who told me that every day. At first I didn't know how to deal with it."

"Did you ever?"

"I did, eventually. She cooked for me and prayed for me, talked and yelled at me."

"Sounds like love."

"Listen to this, the Wyzeckis took me out to dinner at graduation. They gave me some money and a scrapbook." With visible effort, he contained himself. "Turns out Mrs. Wy had been clipping stories about me in the paper for years. My dad had never done that. Fact is, I'm not ready for anything to happen to Mrs. Wy, Minnie."

"I'm not, either."

They looked at each other with new understanding. Matt wasn't a star quarterback. She was no longer the shy, pudgy shadow of her sister. They were both older and wiser, and cared about a lot more things than silly romances and reputations.

"Kimber needs time and patience. That's all."

"Then she's in luck, because that's something I've got in abundance."

"You've got more than that in abundance, Min."

Just like that, awareness clicked in. Oh, she both hated and longed for comments like that from Matt. She wanted to hear them, but she also almost needed him to decipher the meanings. Did he find her attractive? Did he, too, catch himself thinking about taking things a step or two farther?

Okay, a whole lot farther.

He stood up and put some space between them. "I'll start the salad."

A chore sounded good. "Sure. I'll make some tea. And check on Kimber. She can help me set the table."

They parted, unsure of each other. Unsure of what was going to happen to the two of them. Unsure of anything but their pasts.

As Minnie walked toward Kimber, the little girl scrambled to sit up. "Minnie, look at what George can do!" she said, holding poor George in a death grip. As Minnie sat down and watched the guinea pig crawl into the pillow fort Kimber had made him, she realized that time and hope might be exactly what each of them needed.

Chapter Seventeen

Three nights later, Jackie came back late, her lips red and her face flushed. She was creeping through the living room when Matt spoke from Jim's worn easy chair. "Hey, Jackie."

She jumped. "You jerk! You took two years off of me. What are you doing, sitting here in the dark?"

"Sorry. I just turned off the TV." Feeling vaguely paternal, he said, "So, did you have a good time?"

After pausing to lay her purse at the foot of the stairs, Jackie came in, slipped off her shoes and sat across from him. "I did. Lane took me out for barbecue."

"By the looks of your shirt, I'd say he did more than that."

Jackie looked down at her wrinkled blouse and chuckled. "You'd be right. I like him, Matt."

"I thought as much."

"I told him I might start coming out here often."

"Really?" He knew Lane well and liked him a lot. But, well, Matt had never actually thought that Jackie and Lane were a good match. Jackie was all city girl and type A. Lane seemed happy to live in the country and stay close to his roots. "Y'all are that serious?"

"Maybe. I like seeing him, and he makes me happy. He's so different than the men I usually date."

"Anyone would be an improvement after Keith." Matt had only seen him from the distance, but the metro-sexual-looking guy would have been as out of place in their Texas town as, well, Jackie.

"That's true. However, it turns out Lane and I have a lot in common. We realized that as soon as we got through the whole bidding war nightmare."

That had been tough. For a few days, Lane had looked at him like he was the grim reaper. "But then?"

"But then I found myself thinking about him more often than not." She flipped a chunk of hair back over her shoulder. "You know how it goes…opposites attract. Kind of like you and Minnie."

"Minnie and me?" That zinger hit him hard, because Matt knew she was right. He was attracted to Minnie. But he was also smart enough to realize that a serious, long-lasting future between them was aeons away. Their circumstances were not going to change. Store 35 could very well hurt her business and she was going to blame him for that. "We're just friends."

"I've seen the way you two look at each other, and those looks have nothing to do with friendship. Lane's seen the sparks between you, too." Jackie winked. "Plus…Mrs. Wyzecki told me she heard y'all kissed the other day."

That had been some kiss. "It was just for show."

"Uh-huh."

"Kisses aside, I doubt Minnie and I will ever have a future that involves more than friendship. Every time things settle between us, our businesses get in the way."

"Matt, hasn't life taught you anything yet? Work is

great. Work is what gets me up in the morning. But it's not what I want to think about when I go to bed every night. Do you?"

Matt didn't want to even think about Jackie going to bed at night. "I don't know."

"Oh, Matt. You can't plan a future that's only full of promotions and eighty-hour work weeks. Work can't love you back. Sooner or later you're going to have to reach out and grab hold of something that will hold you tight. Something that's flesh and blood."

Work can't love you back.

Long after Jackie had picked up her shoes and walked upstairs, her words echoed in his mind. Matt knew she was right. But he also didn't know what he would do if he for once grabbed hold of someone and she left him.

He didn't know if he had any smiles and swaggers left to cover up the hurt that was sure to come.

Chapter Eighteen

"I should have known better than to have expected so much from Matthew Madigan," Cora Jean Hardt pronounced as clear as day as she picked a chipped frame out of Carried Away's discount bin and studied it for further flaws.

Minnie kept doing what she needed to do—count change and straighten the counter. But that didn't stop her from listening.

Zenia, Cora's sister-in-law for well on thirty years, frowned as she picked up a bent bookmark and studied it. "What did you expect, Cora Jean? After all, his dad was a cold man. I can't hardly ever remember him smiling."

"That's only because Michelle died so young. Now Michelle Madigan was a good sort." Cora Jean sniffed. "Can't say that young Matthew takes after her, though."

Minnie stopped trying to pretend that she wasn't eavesdropping. Sweet as pie, she interrupted. "Miss Zenia, Miss Cora, I'm sorry, but I couldn't help but overhear. What's going on with Matt Madigan?"

One looked at the other. Then they both faced her on

pivoted heels. "We were just discussing—privately, by the way—what Matt Madigan has done."

Last Minnie had heard, Matt was the Easter Bunny and Santa Claus, all wrapped into one extremely good-looking package. "I don't know what Matt has done. Besides move here and open up SavNGo."

"Isn't that enough? Minnie Clark, Matt is ruining our town," Zenia stated.

Cora Jean nodded importantly. "Almost single-handedly, to boot. Quite a number of people's liveli-hoods are on the line, just because he wants a profit!"

"What's happening now?"

"I heard from Lane Henderson's mama that Matt made everyone who had contracts with SavNGo rebid if they wanted that giant of a retailer's business."

"I'd heard about that, but I thought things settled down."

"They settled, but nobody's happy." Zenia picked up a scented candle, stuck her nose deep inside, like a honeybee, then set it back down with a look of distaste. "Yes, indeed. SavNGo has fallen on hard times."

"Well, they can join the club. Abel and Brenda and I have been talking about what is going to happen if things get worse around our town."

"We heard you've been pretty angry. We like the signs y'all posted, too. SOS—Support Our Stores."

Minnie had been pretty proud of them herself. So far, lots of people were coming in to tell her that they wouldn't forget her store even when the mighty con-glomerate came to town. Abel had put the signs out the evening Wanda went into the hospital. And boy, had he been busy! Just yesterday Minnie noticed you could hardly go anywhere without bright green-and-white signs listing names of local businesses.

The ladies had just kept on talking. "They have gotten worse, dear," said Zenia. "Both of Emma Watson's sons got laid off because of his stinginess."

Cora Jean leveled a look Minnie's way. "Emma's youngest needed that job, too, you know."

"I imagine he did." Thinking about how much she needed her business, Minnie added, "What's he going to do now?"

Zenia cast a sharp eye her way over a pair of sparkly teal half-moon readers. "I don't know. Minnie, I was pleased as punch when I heard big business was coming to our town, but now I'm worried."

"I've been worried, too. I hope you'll still come here to shop even when SavNGo comes."

"Don't be silly, Minnie. Of course, we'll still come here. Why, I wouldn't be surprised if nobody even went to SavNGo at all."

Cora Jean picked up another candle and set it on the counter before opening up her checkbook. "Well, thank goodness Lane Henderson still got the work. Pretty much everyone else did, too—they're just not getting paid quite as much as they'd hoped."

"Well, that is something, I suppose."

Zenia nodded. "I agree. After all, what choice do you have when you're in between a rock and a hard place?"

Minnie knew there weren't many choices, not really. Which brought up a tiny, nagging doubt. Maybe Matt didn't have as many choices as she'd imagined he did, after all.

And even though she'd privately called Matt a whole lot worse things, now that she knew his heart was in the right place, she came to his defense.

Just a little, tiny bit.

Zenia plopped her heavy handbag on Minnie's counter with a thump. "I hope Matthew feels horrible about all the trouble SavNGo is causing."

"Maybe Matt is just doing what he was told to do."

"Why *not* blame Matt? He's the voice of that monstrosity in this town," Zenia stated. "And here Wanda's in the hospital." Cora Jean fanned her face with one of Minnie's cards, bending the cardboard with her quick-as-lightning motions. "Poor Wanda. Why, if I was her, I could hardly bring myself to get out of bed."

"That's probably why he picked such a time to do this. Because Wanda couldn't rein him in."

Oh, these ladies were driving her crazy! "Matt's real worried about Wanda. You know he loves her." She nodded toward their hands. "Can I start ringing you up?"

Cora Jean pushed her bounty forward on the counter. "Yes, please, Minnie. Thank goodness we can depend on you."

"And to think we were once so excited about discount wrapping paper," Zenia exclaimed.

They bought even more than usual. Minnie tried to feel enthusiastic about how their purchases would help the day's sales, but it was leaving a bad taste in her mouth. She didn't like to hear such strong words about Matt.

If word got out that he was disliked so much, Minnie knew he'd be devastated.

THE MACHINES IN THE ROOM made a metal gasping noise every time Mrs. Wyzecki took a breath. Matt leaned forward on his elbows and tried not to breathe right there with her. It took concentration not to—watching her in the faded blue print hospital gown, looking pale after her surgery, made him want to hold his breath. He was worried about her, and he'd hardly left her bedside since she'd come out of recovery.

The truth was, Matt was so scared about losing Wanda that he felt he was slowly losing a part of himself with each laborious inhale and exhale.

"I promise, Matt. It may not look like it, but she's recovering just fine," Dr. Garcia said when he stuck his head in. "The surgery went well. She's going to be feeling a lot better soon."

"She doesn't look good."

"I fixed her heart, Matt. Give the rest of her time to adjust. She'll be ordering us around before long."

Matt nodded as he breathed along with Wanda. In. Out. In. Out.

Another hour passed. He'd just drifted to sleep when Wanda's scratchy voice brought him upright in a matter of seconds.

"Some people sleep in beds, don't you know."

"Ha-ha. Some people don't make others worry so much."

"Oh, Matthew. You'd have years of pacing to catch up with the worrying I've done over you."

Matt had no doubt that was true. "How are you feeling?"

"I'd be better if you'd lean back in that chair. I can hardly take a breath without feeling you hovering over me."

Gently, he rubbed her arm while moving back a bit. "Sorry. I didn't know you were awake."

"I wasn't until I heard you snoring."

He'd never snored in his life. "Sorry. I'll, uh, try and settle down."

"Good." Her eyes narrowed. "Don't you be getting all emotional on me, Matthew."

"Never that. So will you ever answer me? How are you feeling?"

"Not so good. Actually, I feel like someone's taken a sledgehammer to my body, I'm so sore." Fastening pale blue eyes his way, she said, "How are things going with you?"

"Fine."

"I can still go to that care center, you know."

"Not yet you can't."

"Matthew—"

"We'll talk about it when you're better."

Derisively, she scanned him up and down. "You're a liar, Matthew. I don't think you're going to want to talk about me moving anytime. And if your sad expression is any indication, I don't think you're fine, either."

"You're mistaken."

"Humph. How's Minnie?"

"She's all right. Taking care of Kimber."

"Well, that's pretty much a full-time job for a team of people, let alone one Minnie Clark. I imagine that Minnie could use someone sturdy to lean on." She took a break as the machine did its thing. "Maybe you could let her lean on you for a bit."

"I've been doing my best." Though their dinner and the fish funeral had been sweet, he'd seen very little of Minnie since.

Matt also couldn't help but notice the SOS signs that dotted almost every corner in their town. Those green-and-white signs, together with some general disgruntlement about the rebidding hadn't done him or SavNGo any favors.

Wanda looked at him anxiously. "But you'll try to look after Minnie? She needs you."

What could he say? "Yes, ma'am. Of course I'll try."

MATT THOUGHT about his conversation with Mrs. Wy a bit more when he got back into the truck and headed out to the work site. More concrete was due to be poured this week, and on Friday, he needed to fly back to the home office and attend a series of meetings.

The first person he saw when he got to the trailer was Lane. His friend was dressed in his usual attire, ball cap, jeans, work boots and wrinkled button-downs. What wasn't familiar was the look of regret on his friend's face. "Hey."

"You got a minute?"

"You know I do," Matt said.

They walked into the trailer and Matt cranked up the air. So far, September wasn't turning out to be much cooler than August. "Have a seat?"

"Nah. I'd rather stand for this."

Matt's stomach was churning. What in the world had he done now?

"See, it's like this. After speaking with Jackie, I decided that I owe you an apology."

"There's nothing to apologize for."

"Yeah, there is. I was pretty angry with you when you told me the news about the bids. I gave you a hard time."

"I thought we already made up."

"Matt, I don't want you to think that the only reason we're okay is because I got the bid again."

Matt figured that was what had happened. "But you think differently?"

"Jackie got me thinking about change, and with change comes the good and the bad. I had forgotten that."

Stuffing his hands in his back pockets, Lane added, "Jackie also reminded me that you are only doing the best you can. She told me some stories about the VIPs at SavNGo."

"I made mistakes, too. I should've warned you that things like this had happened before. And, well, I could have explained myself better, I guess. So...we good?"

Lane shook the hand he offered. "We're good. How's the packing coming along? Do you need any help?"

"You're welcome to help, but it's going slow. Now that I'm trying to get things ready for Wanda to move back there's stuff everywhere."

"How about I come over tonight and help you for a bit?"

Matt smiled gratefully. "Thanks."

Lane turned to go, but before he did, he stopped and turned back. "You know, sometimes when times are hardest, it's best to hold close the people you can count on."

"I hear you."

"Minnie Clark is one of the finest women I know," Lane said. "She's got a lot of good qualities."

Matt was getting uncomfortable. Why was Lane telling him all this? He already knew that Minnie had good qualities.

But Lane kept talking, like he was the guest on a daytime talk show. "Minnie cares about people, Matt. She cares about their successes...and failures. She always has. I wouldn't be too hard on her about those signs popping up everywhere. She's only doing what she thinks she has to do."

When Lane opened the trailer's door, a handful of dust floated in, capturing Matt's attention. When it cleared and Lane was gone, Matt thought he could finally see things clearly.

Minnie and he did have a mess of differences, but they had a lot in common, too. And once more, there was an understanding between them that was comforting. Neither expected too much from the other.

Actually, Matt reckoned that neither expected much from anyone, which was really kind of a crying shame.

Chapter Nineteen

Minnie was busier than ever. In order to stay sane, she'd begun to stop thinking ahead and started taking her own advice—concentrate on one thing at a time.

It wasn't very easy.

Each day, Minnie met with local artists in an effort to sell more of their crafts, worked in the store, and took care of Kimber. She hired additional help at Carried Away so she could spend more time running her niece to playdates and her Brownie meetings. Though the thought of not having her hand in every transaction at the store bothered her, not doing justice to her niece was a far greater concern.

And at the moment, Kimber's reading lesson was at the top of the list.

Minnie was sure that she must have done something very wrong when she was younger and she was being punished now with the grief she was getting studying with Kimber. Each homework assignment was a battle, each study session a war of wills.

Minnie knew she was going to start drinking at noon if things didn't get easier soon.

"Listen, we've got to learn the words in this book,"

Minnie said as they sat next to each other at the kitchen table. "Mrs. Strickland wants you to be able to read *Dog and Frog* out loud by the end of the month."

"I don't want to."

"You're out of choices. Now I'm here to help you, but you've gotta do your part."

Kimber glared at the book, opened her mouth, shook her head and finally spoke. "I can't learn the words. They're too hard."

"Oh, sweetheart." There it was. Just like a slice of sun after a month of cloudy days, Kimber was finally breaking through.

Ever since her niece had come to live with her, anything that was difficult or uncomfortable had thrown Kimber into a tailspin. Instead of verbalizing what the problem was, Kimber had found it easier to argue and whine. Refuse and cry. And get angry.

Oh, she'd been so angry. Minnie had dealt with the torrents of emotion the best she could, visiting counselors and reading all about grief and loss. But she hadn't needed a parenting book to tell her what she knew in her heart—Kimber was angry because she missed her mom and dad. She was angry and petulant because she wanted some control.

Treading carefully, Minnie said, "I don't know if that's the truth. Mrs. Strickland seemed to think this book was just your speed. Can't we try it again?"

Kimber stared at *Dog and Frog* with fierce longing, so tangible that Minnie could feel it. "Other kids can already read this book," Kimber said, her voice thin and full of embarrassment. "Most everybody else in the whole class can."

"That doesn't mean a thing. All that matters is what

you can do. Take it from me, comparing yourself to other people gets you in trouble every time."

"What do you mean?"

Minnie scooted closer to Kimber, who for once had stopped swinging her legs against the legs of the chair. "I used to compare myself to your mother all the time."

"Mommy?"

"Yep. She was the prettiest girl I knew. And she had lots of friends. Paige was smart, too. Really smart. Sometimes I was sure she could get an A on a test just by holding the book under her arm."

"But not you?"

"No. Not me. I wanted to be just like Paige. Oh, I tried to be just like her."

Wide brown eyes met that news. "Were you?"

"Nope. I was too shy. Too awkward. I was good at math, not at drama and music." Minnie couldn't help but smile at the memories. Oh, to think she'd actually tried out for the cheerleading squad! She, the master introvert! "I wasn't a good 'Paige' at all. Instead, I learned to be a good 'Minnie.'"

That pronouncement brought a hesitant smile. "I like Minnie."

"I'm glad. And guess what? I like *Kimber.* I feel certain that we are going to be able to read a couple of words in this book before you know it. If we don't give up."

Next to her shoulder, Minnie felt Kimber relax. Thank goodness she'd finally said the right thing. Slowly opening the book, she folded the title page back. Together she and Kimber pointed to the first word on the page, just like Mrs. Strickland had showed them to do. "Run."

Kimber followed along. They read some more. "Fun. In. The. Sun."

Wide eyes peeked up at her. "*Fun* and *sun* rhyme."

"Yep." Minnie gave Kimber a little squeeze. "You are exactly right."

They read some more and cheered together when Kimber recognized *fun* and *run* on another page. Progress had been made in more ways than one.

Twenty minutes later, Minnie closed the book, feeling more at peace than she could recall in a while. "What would you like to do now?"

Kimber hopped off her chair as if it were on fire. "See Matt?" She pointed out the window. "Look, Minnie. He's sitting on Mrs. Wy's steps. We can just walk over."

Minnie had been doing her best to avoid him since she saw him scowling at the SOS sign she had planted next to the stop sign at the front of their street.

But she was curious about Wanda, and did want to try to patch things up. No matter what happened between them, Minnie couldn't ignore the fact that she had a soft spot for Matt Madigan, and probably always would.

With Kimber for company, Minnie crossed the street. Matt was lounging on the old rocking chair of Wanda's—the one that looked like a big wind would break it in two. A mason jar filled with iced tea was beside him. He stood up when they approached. "Good afternoon, ladies. What brings you my way?"

"We've been reading," Kimber said importantly.

Matt peeked at Minnie.

It's a big deal, she mouthed over Kimber's head.

That famous movie-star grin appeared. "Well, that's about the best news I've ever heard," Matt said. "Tell me all about it."

"I can read some of my book. Minnie helped." Kimber picked up the hose that was in a messy pile at the side of the house. "Can I water your flowers? Mrs. Wy lets me do it sometimes."

They all looked at the bed of begonias. The batches of red and fuchsia pink flowers were shriveling and wilted.

Minnie couldn't resist teasing him. "Conserving water, Matt?"

"Obviously. Kimber, I think watering those flowers would be a real good idea."

Eager to please, she jumped from foot to foot. "I could water tomorrow, too."

"I think you should water all you want. These plants need some serious help."

When Kimber turned the corner and was out of earshot, Minnie sat down on the other rocker. "So, how are things going?"

He shrugged. "I don't know. Okay, I guess. Mrs. Wy got an infection so she's not home yet."

"Anything I can do?"

"Not yet. Maybe when she gets here, you could help me keep tabs on her."

"I can do that."

After another pause, Matt cleared his throat. "So, how's your SOS sign campaign?"

"Successful, as a matter of fact." Minnie could feel her cheeks heat, but she soldiered on. No way was she going to be embarrassed for trying everything she could to keep her store afloat. "Business is pretty good."

"I'm glad. I never wanted to hurt your business, Min."

"You know what? I actually believe you now."

"Well, that's something, I guess."

As Kimber moved to another flower bed, carefully

tending to each flower, Matt leaned back on his palms. "We're a real pair, aren't we? Sitting here, holding so many worries inside."

"On the outside, we look just fine, though."

Matt chuckled. "Yeah, I've always been good at that. On the outside, I can make everything seem just fine."

After a moment, Minnie changed the subject. "Did I hear that Jackie is just about to go back to Philadelphia?"

"Yep. She helped me with the latest round of bidding and get through a pile of paperwork, but her job is there. Lane took her out tonight."

"They sure hit it off."

"They did."

"I can see why. Jackie is so bright and cheerful. I've never seen anyone so small do so much."

"She's a Tasmanian devil. People either gravitate to her or run like hell."

"I kind of felt like doing both."

"Me, too, at times." He looked at her then. Really looked. "I know you're worried about Carried Away and that more often than not we end up snipping at each other. But…would you like to go out with me on Saturday night?"

"Like a date?"

"Yeah." He looked at his hands for a moment. "It, uh, might be fun."

"It does sound like fun. Thank you."

"Good. I'll pick you up at seven. Maybe we could go to the movies or dinner."

"I'd like that. I'll ask Mom or Dad if they could watch Kimber."

A sweet smile played on the edge of his lips just before Kimber came rushing over and accidentally sprayed them both with cold water. "Yikes!" he said, standing up in a flash.

Kimber dropped the hose. "I'm sorry, I didn't mean to!"

Matt clambered down the steps. "Kimber, you know what happens to little girls who spray old men, don't you?"

Her eyes wide and worried, she froze. "What?"

"They get sprayed right back." With lightning speed, Matt grabbed the hose, stuck his thumb over the opening, then pointed it Kimber's direction. As the wide arch of water skimmed her shoes, the little girl yelped. And then she ran toward him. Matt complied and sprayed her again. She squealed with delight.

And then the race was on. Minnie stayed dry on the porch and watched the two of them chase each other with the hose. Getting soaked. Trampling on those poor, almost withered begonias.

Laughing.

Somehow, Minnie didn't think Wanda would mind.

Chapter Twenty

"Well, I guess we can't say that punctuality isn't your strong point," Minnie said brightly when she opened the door. "The clock just chimed seven."

"Yeah. Well." Yep, that was the extent of Matt's witty comeback. But it wasn't his fault. Matt was truly, honest-to-God struck dumb.

Who knew Minnie could wear a dress so well? She had on some kind of sleeveless silky dress, all in a nubby violet. The soft color brought out the pink in her cheeks and the brown of her eyes.

On a less-endowed girl, the dress might have looked a little boxy. Maybe even unattractive. On Minnie, however, it moved and swayed with her figure, hugging her chest and hips. Those black patent leather high heels hadn't gone unnoticed, either. Her legs looked long and pretty.

And with her thick hair pulled back into a simple ponytail, Matt was torn between admiring how nice it was to see all of her face and the desire to watch her hair fall back around her shoulder blades.

Stepping out, she turned and locked the door behind her. Then she looked at him quizzically. "Matt? Anything wrong?"

"Not a thing." Except for the fact that he was tongue-tied. He shook his head to clear it. Held out a hand to help her down the steps. "Let's go."

A flash of hurt entered her eyes before she nodded. "All right."

Now it was too late to say a word about her appearance. If he said something now, it would come off as an obligation to say the right thing. Instead, he slid one hand around her elbow and placed his other lightly around her hip, holding her steady as she hoisted herself into the cab of his truck.

After he got in on his own side and began to drive, he glanced Minnie's way again. Raspberry-colored lip gloss shone on her lips. Dangling purple stones hung from her ears. A silver charm bracelet decorated her wrist.

And though it was probably too late, he said the words anyway. "You look real pretty, Minnie. Smell good, too."

"Thanks, Matt."

She crossed her legs. The dress scooted up an inch, revealing a portion of thigh encased in silky stocking. Even though he'd seen just as much leg in her shorts, he was still tempted to stare. Imagined running a hand down those legs, just to see how she'd respond.

It was a good thing he could focus on the road.

After dinner, when they were standing in line for movie tickets, Minnie kept looking at the poster in front of them. "I can't believe we're going to pay so much to watch *Creature from the Blue Lagoon*."

He leaned in closer just so he could watch her blush. "You're missin' the point. Nobody goes to a movie like this expecting to see a plot."

"I suppose. I just hope it's not too scary."

"I think the bad guy is covered in swamp water, Min.

You'll be able to handle it. Especially since I'll be sitting right beside you."

Sure enough, the creature was right out of B-movie bad guys. He was tortured and scary, and seemed to take a lot of joy strangling people with seaweed.

Matt would have broken down and laughed if Minnie hadn't been sitting so frightened next to him.

Instead, he concentrated on keeping her mind off the movie. That, of course, meant a whole lot of kissing, hand holding and a certain amount of eye covering when the heroine got sucked into the swamp.

She was still shivering from the especially bloody ending when they walked out to the parking lot. "I don't know if I'm ever going to trust you again to choose a movie, Matt."

"You will," he said, opening the truck door for her. "Come on, wasn't it a little bit fun to be scared?"

Her cheeks bloomed, as she obviously remembered their kisses and not the swamp monster. "A little."

AND JUST AS SHE HAD many times before, Minnie found herself falling under his spell. She couldn't help but notice how good his arms looked underneath the ultra-fine cotton of his shirt. Shoot, she couldn't resist how well he was dressed, for that matter.

And those eyes, those God-given glorious blue eyes. That dark hair, cut so short, catching her eye. Making her wonder what it would feel like under her hands.

"Tonight's been fun."

"I thought so, too. We ought to do this more often."

Do what more often? Dine out? Flirt in public? Forget everything between them and just concentrate on now? "I agree."

She noticed he still hadn't buckled his seat belt. Night had come and the sky was dim, shadowing other people in the tree-covered parking lot. The sky was cooler, and the temperature inside the truck cab was comfortable.

He shifted, scooting a good bit closer, turning his body so they were almost sitting at right angles. Reaching out, he linked his fingers with hers.

His hand felt good in hers. Solid and warm.

Matt swallowed, his eyes on her face. Scanning her features, he seemed to be memorizing what she looked like. "You look so pretty tonight, and not just because of that dress, which, I really hope you won't wear for another man because it's going to make me jealous as sin. You look so pretty because of your glow. The way you smile. The way you make me feel good inside." He leaned closer, his lips only inches away from hers. "The way you make me want to kiss you again."

Then he did just that.

A sweet brush of lips melded into a heart-stopping contact, effectively robbing Minnie of her breath and grasping hold of him for balance.

Matt easily complied. He tilted his head and held her closer. Whispered sweet words just before they got busy again. But this time their kisses had nothing to do with hesitant tastes.

Or schoolgirl daydreams. This time their kisses were intimate and carnal. Sure hands slid behind Minnie's back, moved her closer to his chest. The hem of her dress slid high as she was pulled onto his lap. And then all kinds of sensations rushed forward.

The scrape of starched denim under silk-covered legs. The crisp scent of cotton from Matt's shirt. His cologne. His cheeks, lightly stubbled. The calluses on his fingertips, brushing across her chest, igniting her senses, causing her breasts to feel lifted, heavy, aching for his touch.

His taste, like Matt.

The roar of a car's ignition and embarrassed laughter of the couple next to them brought reality back.

Startled, Minnie pulled away, scrambling to straighten her dress.

The vehicle pulled out of the parking lot just as Matt carefully slid two fingers inside the V of her neckline and set it to rights. Lord help her. All she wanted was to feel his fingers on her bare skin.

His hand dropped away. "Are you okay?"

"Of course." Minnie smoothed her skirt back over her thigh and tried to sit like a lady.

Matt turned on the ignition. The burst of air should have been cooling but it seemed to only fan her sensitized skin. Matt closed his eyes for a moment. "Jeez, Minnie. How about I take you home? I'm too old to do this in a car."

Taking a deep breath, Minnie said, "Matt, I should really let you know something. I...I've liked you for quite a while. Since when you dated Paige. Even with everything that's going on with my business and your job, I can't deny the truth. I have strong feelings for you. But I'd still like to take things slow."

Well, there it was. Yet another skeleton in the cupboard that had been sprung.

To her surprise, Matt didn't look surprised or off-kilter. Something just slid into those eyes of his as he put the truck in Reverse. And as they entered the highway, he lifted up an arm. "Any chance you want to slide on over here while we drive on home, just like the kids in high school do?"

"You're not upset?" While he seemed to be taking everything in stride, Minnie was finding herself even more off balance than usual.

"Not at all." As they pulled out onto the highway, Matt twirled a lock of hair around two fingers. "We've waited a long time to even get this far, Minnie. I think we can wait a while longer for anything else. Don't you?"

In reply, Minnie scooted a little closer and rested her head against his shoulder.

Chapter Twenty-One

"She is so hot," Lane said, for what seemed like the fiftieth time. "Don't you think she's smoking?"

Matt glanced at Jackie's business card held securely in Lane's hand. SavNGo Corporation was so big that human resources encouraged photos on business cards. And though at first Matt had balked at the concept, he had to admit that the idea had merit. After looking at people's names and faces in his Rolodex, it became a lot easier to recognize members of the workforce.

But for the life of him, Matt had never seen a person stare at a photo like Lane was doing with Jackie's. "She's my personal assistant. I don't think of her like that. When are you going to believe me?"

"I believe you. I just haven't felt this way about anyone before. I'm having trouble handling it."

"You don't look like it. You look like you're happy as a clam."

"A lot goes on inside a person that you can't always see," Lane replied sagely.

"I suppose." Matt recalled the many times he'd struggled to look calm and confident while staring at

Minnie's signs or coming face-to-face with general resentment in Abel Pierce's hardware store.

The afternoon Minnie and Kimber had stopped by had been one of the few times he'd felt like giving in to his blues. It had almost been a relief to reveal his weaknesses…if only for a little while.

Perhaps that was why Minnie was becoming so important to him. He could be weak with her…and she never backed down.

Picking up the pace, they strode to the construction site. After receiving the standard bright yellow hard hats, they began taking notes and figuring out the latest glitch in the schedule. No SavNGo had ever gone up according to plan. But this one was pretty damn close. So far everything was going so right it was almost eerie. Matt had fallen asleep more than one night with his cell phone next to him, half-waiting for something dire to explode.

But so far, nothing had happened.

"What has she said about me?"

"She likes you."

That stopped Lane in his tracks. Looking all goofy, he said, "I knew it."

"Come on. I said she likes you. That's it. Don't get all high school on me."

"I'm not. So what else? Does she think I'm cute?"

She did, but there was no way Matt was going to start reporting that. Already he felt weird. "I don't know."

"Come on. She's got to have said more."

"Not much more. I know you can't believe it, but Jackie and I don't sit around discussing personal lives when we talk. We discuss work. Finally, even if we did discuss personal things, Jackie would never say a thing about you to me, that's why. We don't have that kind of relationship."

Lane didn't take the hint. Still fingering that damned card like a stalker, he said, "You should get to know Jackie better. She'd be a good friend, you know?"

What could Matt say to that? "I don't need another friend."

Lane almost smiled. "If you counted Jackie's friendship, you'd almost have a handful of people who you let get close to you. Wouldn't that be something?"

It would be something, all right.

Chapter Twenty-Two

"Mrs. Wy said she's getting better," Kimber informed Minnie the moment they walked in Minnie's house. Matt had volunteered to pick up Kimber and let her visit with Wanda for a while. "The doctor said she's gonna come home in a couple of days."

"Maybe," Matt corrected. "Mrs. Wyzecki might get to come home soon. She's recovering well from the angioplasty and everyone expects her to make a full recovery."

Minnie couldn't resist hugging Matt. Wanda meant so much to both of them. "That's great news."

Pressing a kiss to the top of her head, Matt leaned in close. "It sure is. I can't wait until we can go back to how things were."

Minnie was contemplating that statement when Kimber came over and wrapped her arms around Minnie, too. "That's from Mrs. Wy."

Getting down on her knees, Minnie held out her arms. "Do you have any hugs in there for me?"

"Yep!" Two arms hugged tight.

"You made my day with your news and your hugs."

When they separated, Kimber said, "I'm going to go see George and put on my princess pajamas."

"I'll tuck you into bed in a few minutes, so start thinking of a book," Minnie said, then finally looked at Matt. He was standing against the wall, one leg crossed over the other, chewing on a piece of gum.

She walked toward him. "So, how is Wanda, really?"

"Really? She's better than I thought she could be. She also was griping about her new diet. For a lady whose best friend was butter, it's going to be a bit of a change."

"I'll help with that. It's just such a relief to know that she's going to be home soon." Minnie gestured toward the couch. "Would you like to stay for a while? After I get Kimber off to bed?"

Within seconds Matt's expression transformed from concerned friend and neighbor to vintage sexy-as-sin Matt Madigan. The same expression that had always caused her to shiver. "Yeah. I'd like to stay. I'll, uh, pour us some wine."

"I'll be right back."

To her surprise, the usual bedtime routine took five minutes instead of twenty. Kimber was tired and happy to be in bed, thanks to her new pajamas. After quickly saying prayers for Paige, Jeremy, Mrs. Wy, George and Mr. Orange Fish, Minnie hugged Kimber then closed the door behind her.

Matt stood up when she entered and handed Minnie a half-filled glass. "Here you go. Here's to another week."

"And what a week it was. I thought it would never end."

"You and me, both."

"Let's not talk about work." He sipped from his wineglass, then set it on the table. Lowering his voice, he reached for her, draping an arm around her shoulders, and leaned in closer. "I missed you. I kept thinking about our movie date."

"I've thought about that a lot, too. It was fun."

Playing with the ends of her hair, he brushed a few strands out of the way and nibbled on her earlobe. "We'll have to go to the movies again. Soon."

A ripple of desire jumped through her as Matt explored her neck. "I'm not seeing another scary one."

"We can watch whatever you want. Shoot, we can do whatever you want, honey." Just as he claimed her lips, he murmured, "Anything."

Oh, she loved the way he made her feel so special. And, well, he was sure talented. Not many men could massage a girl's neck and kiss her senseless the way he was doing. Making her feel all loose and languid and warm.

His hands on the top button of her blouse, he murmured, "So, you sure Kimber's asleep?"

"Pretty sure."

He moved to the second button. "Good." After another lengthy set of kisses, Minnie's shirt was undone, she felt hot and bothered and Matt looked ready to do a whole lot more than just kiss on the couch.

Because Minnie was thinking the same thing—well, almost—she supposed she had better make sure things were clear between them. "Matt?"

Matt was playing with her hair. "Hmm?"

"This is real nice…and I want to be with you, but well, when I said me and Peter waited, that I've been waiting…I meant well…"

"You're a virgin?"

"Well, yes."

And there it was. Out in the open. Sitting there. Almost mortifying.

Matt raised an eyebrow, obviously waiting for the other shoe to drop. "I kind of figured that, Min."

No, make that *completely mortifying*.

"I thought you did. But, well, I didn't want you to be disappointed before…"

Matt still looked bemused. "Before I jumped you?"

"This is really embarrassing, I hope you know."

He ran one finger down to the base of her neck. "You're blushing. Why are you embarrassed?"

"Because I'm twenty-four."

Matt's blue eyes sparkled. "Is that too young or too old?"

Grabbing a pillow from behind her back, she tossed it at him. "Matt Madigan, I can't believe you're teasing me about this." But inside, she was relieved he was teasing her. With any other man, Minnie knew the conversation would be even more awkward.

He easily fended off her attack. With a light thud, the pillow fell at their feet. His lips twitched. "I'm sorry. I don't mean to embarrass you. Why haven't you ever— were you scared?"

"No. I…I hate to talk bad about Paige. But she was, you know…"

Matt supplied the words. "A little free and easy?"

She nodded. "I heard all the rumors."

A dark look entered his eyes. "Some of them were true."

"I know." During sophomore year, after discovering a boy had only asked her out because he'd thought she would be easy like Paige, Minnie had made a vow. "At first, I just wanted to wait. And then, well, then there wasn't anyone special. And then there was Peter."

Matt rolled his eyes. "Peter."

"I got it into my mind that since I'd waited so long—"

"Almost twenty-four years," Matt supplied.

"Yes, well, that since I'd waited so long, I'd wait until my wedding night." She closed her eyes, remembering that conversation. "I thought Peter would be all for that."

"Any man would be." Amusement flashed in his eyes again. If there was anything Matt could do, it was see humor in any situation. "As long as the engagement was a short one."

"Actually, Peter didn't exactly respond the way I'd thought he would."

Amusement gone, Matt reached for her hand and linked his fingers through hers. "He didn't take your news to heart?"

She tried to smile. "He didn't even take it to his big toe. Peter didn't…" She swallowed, trying to come up with the right way to phrase things. "Peter thought…"

With a quick tug, Matt pulled her closer. She repositioned herself in his arms. "What? That there was something wrong with you?"

Thankful her face was hidden against his chest, Minnie nodded. "Peter started thinking that since no one else had wanted me, that maybe he shouldn't, either."

"I'm confused. I thought he broke up with you because of Kimber."

"Partly." Remembering the whole horrible exchange that had taken only twenty minutes but felt like a whole day, Minnie pulled away and looked at Matt. "Peter didn't want another man's daughter. But he also told me that he was sure he could do better than me."

"Better than a woman who'd saved herself for him." Matt let out a bark of laughter. "Jeez, Minnie. What an ass! He's a fool."

She wasn't sure if he was laughing at the situation or at her antiquated values. Peter—and a lifetime of

going up against Paige and being found lacking—
had taken its toll. "Matt, let's not talk about this any
longer."

"Sorry, but we might as well continue on. We're
neck-deep in this conversation now. Min, Peter's an
idiot for not seeing what you're offering—and what
you've been saving—as a gift."

His words brought her hope. Unexpected and bright
and shining. "So, it doesn't bother you?"

"Hell, no." He flashed her a crooked smile. "Now,
don't be mad, but when you kind of hinted around
it…well, I wasn't all that surprised."

"You're not?"

"Nope. You've seemed a little…hesitant. I wasn't
sure if it had to do with me or you."

"It wasn't you." No, everything with Matt had felt so
right.

"Well, now I know."

"So…we're okay?"

"We're fine. It doesn't matter what you've done
before me. I wouldn't have cared if you'd had several
relationships— Lord knows I have. I sure don't think
there's anything wrong with the fact that you haven't.
It's nice. Refreshing."

For the first time in a while, old dreams surfaced
again. "You sure?"

"Positive. Minnie, I like you. And just to let you
know…I want you." He said the last matter-of-factly,
without a hint of embarrassment.

She pressed a hand to her heart. "Oh, my heart's
still beating a mile a minute. I can't tell you how
worried I was."

His eyes followed that hand, settled in right there on her

chest. His sweet, patient easygoing smile faltered. "There's nothing to be worried about, Min. Nothing's changed."

He was wrong. Everything had changed. The way he looked at her felt different. The way she felt when he did was different, too. More heated. Aware.

Now that she'd admitted to him her feelings, she could admit things to herself, too. Fact was, she wanted Matt, bad. Slowly she dropped her hand. Bit her bottom lip. "So. When do you want to—"

He groaned. "Do the deed? How 'bout we take things slow?"

She hadn't managed such a big step forward just to feel they were going three steps back. "I'm not a child."

"Honey, believe me. I realize that. I'm not, either." Matt ran two fingers along the strap of her top, smoothing it over her bra strap, watching his fingers on her.

Minnie trembled.

He swallowed. "I've long since passed the age where I needed anything in a hurry." His hand, so warm, so gently rough, brushed back her hair, then traced the lines of her neck, stopping on her pulse point. "I'm going to kind of like taking things one step at a time. Slowly."

"If that's what you want."

Humor sparked those eyes again as Matt continued to touch her. Now two fingers traced her collarbone. He was learning her body, inch by inch. "God, you are so soft." A muscle jumped in his jaw. "Let's talk about what *you* want. Do you still want to wait for a wedding night?"

She wanted her first time to be with Matt. Sooner than later. Preferably a whole lot sooner. "No."

"You sure? Because I wouldn't hold it against you."

It didn't escape her that Matt wasn't talking about *their* wedding night. He wasn't talking about any commitments at all.

"Then how about we neck a little bit?" Down went those fingers, to her breastbone. Lingering just at the top of her cleavage. "Right here on the couch."

"I'll go check on Kimber real quick," she said, hoping she could convince her body to move away from him.

Satisfaction gleamed as his fingers drifted away, leaving a cool imprint on her skin. "Okay. I'll put on some music."

As she'd hoped, Kimber was sound asleep, her arms thrown over her head. Minnie tucked the covers around her, then tiptoed out of the room.

When she returned to the living room, Matt was sprawled out on the couch. Both feet were still snug in their boots, which were propped up on the coffee table. Just the sight of him sitting there, sprawled out and waiting for her, brought Minnie up short.

Catching her eye, he raised a brow. "Minnie, you coming over?"

In no time, Minnie was in Matt's arms again. This time with two vanilla-scented candles burning on the coffee table and the soft sounds of Tim McGraw singing in the background.

And Minnie felt safe. Matt didn't think she was undesirable or not good enough.

When he cupped her chin and deepened the kiss, she tilted her mouth and invited his tongue in. She shifted easily when he moved, so he was almost lying on top of her, and invited his attentions again.

His kisses became more demanding. Hot. Full of promises. Her body ignited under his touch. His hips pressed into hers, and it was evident that Matt was just as affected as she was.

Brushing his lips along the lines of her jaw, along the whole path where his fingers had been just a while before, Matt held her close, then helped her slip out of that darn button-down shirt. Her bra came off next.

For a moment, Matt looked like he had won the lottery. Then, settled over her breasts, he murmured silly sweet words of appreciation.

She arched her back. He licked a nipple. She pressed him closer. Lifted her hips. Heard Matt groan.

Moments later, looking as if someone was pulling him away, Matt lifted his head and met her gaze. "You're killing me, sugar."

But his blue eyes said something else. They had a glow about them. Like he wasn't dying at all. More like he was enjoying every little thing they were doing together.

And later, after she'd reclaimed her shirt and Matt stood up and grabbed his hat, she felt powerful and beautiful.

"Minnie, I know we said we'd take this slow, but maybe we ought to start rethinking that timetable."

Minnie could honestly say she was in no hurry to put off what she'd been putting off forever. "Whenever you're ready."

"Lord have mercy," he breathed. "You shouldn't say that."

"Why? When will you be ready?"

"Five minutes ago." He rested his forehead on hers and breathed deep. "Let's do some thinking and reconvene in the morning."

He kissed her again and quickly left.

Making Minnie think that for once she'd done everything right after all.

Chapter Twenty-Three

Later that night, in the privacy of his own room back at Mrs. Wyzecki's, Matt acknowledged the truth. While Minnie's admission hadn't caught him off guard, he wasn't quite sure how to move forward.

He'd hadn't met inexperienced girls even in college. For Minnie to be that way, why, it was almost shocking. But not necessarily disappointing.

He thought back to their first kiss. It had been nice. Their second one had, too. So had their little session in his truck. Minnie had been responsive and eager. But there had seemed to be something missing.

A surety. She hadn't pressed against him when he curved his hands around her ass. She hadn't given him a look that promised she was as eager as he was to get naked.

Though a part of him wanted to take her in his arms as soon as possible and get the job done, a saner part thought something more special ought to happen. First times were pretty momentous, and that scared him. He didn't have any experience with that.

There was no one to talk about this with, either. It was special, and secret and too sweet and close to his heart to bring out for general discussion. But he did need a plan.

Minnie needed something fun to break the ice. Matt had a feeling if he brought her straight up to his bed she'd be a nervous wreck. No, she needed something to get them close together but not mess things up.

Something secluded and private. He looked out the window.

What Minnie and he needed was someplace like... here.

TWO DAYS LATER, Matt had finished work for the day, and was sitting on his front porch watching nothing, trying to figure out how to get Minnie to his house without bringing along a certain demanding curly-haired girl. The best person to ask for help in this would be Wanda. But that obviously couldn't happen.

The last time he and Minnie had been on her couch, she had mentioned that she'd asked her parents to watch Kimber overnight sometime soon.

It was too bad that her parents were already booked up for the next two weekends.

Matt was just telling himself that waiting another couple of weeks wasn't going to be too difficult when Kimber's crying brought him up short. "Matt!"

He stood up as she scampered across the street and trotted to him, her black Mary Janes sparkling in the late afternoon sun. "What's wrong, honey?"

She pulled up two feet in front of him, out of breath. "Minnie's not home."

"She's not? Who picked you up from day care?"

"Grandpa and Grandma. They're at Minnie's. But I don't want to talk to them. I got a problem." She reached her hand out to him but then dropped it.

Matt's heart went out to her. He knew exactly what

it was like, wanting so hard to reach for another person but being just as afraid that it would be a big mistake. "Want to talk to me about it?"

"Uh-huh."

Feeling like her knight in armor, Matt held out his hand to her. She gripped it hard. "You can stay with me until Minnie gets back, if you'd like."

After talking to Minnie's parents, and then making a call to Carried Away so Minnie would know where Kimber was, he got her a snack, then took Kimber back out to the front stoop. After sitting beside her on the top step, he stretched out his legs. "Okay, sweetheart. I'm all ears. What's wrong?"

"Nanci Velasquez invited me to her party."

"Well, now. That sounds fun."

Tears sneaked out the corners of her eyes.

He assumed all little girls liked parties. "What's wrong with Nanci?"

"Nothing. Nanci's real nice."

"Well, then?"

Kimber sighed dramatically. "The party's a slumber party."

"Uh-huh?" He really had no experience with girl things. "What's wrong with that?"

"I've never been to one."

"Oh. You scared?"

"Maybe." After a moment, she blurted, "Mommy always said I was too little to sleep anywhere but at home."

"What are you going to do?"

"I don't know. I like Nanci. If I don't go, she might be mad at me."

"That sounds kind of harsh."

"She's my best friend, Matt." Her voice a little lower, Kimber added, "She's one of my only friends."

He didn't know slumber parties, but he did know what it was like, trying to make friends when you didn't quite fit in. "Maybe you could give it a try. You can always call Minnie if you get scared and want to come home early."

"I can do that? You think it's allowed?"

Hoping he wasn't way off the mark, Matt said, "Sure it's allowed."

Visibly struggling, Kimber bit her lip. "I want to go. But Mommy—"

He held up a hand. "When did your mommy say you were too young?"

"A long time ago."

"Things change as people get older. I bet she told you you couldn't get snacks by yourself, or take a bath by yourself, but you can now, can't you?"

She nodded.

"Maybe your mommy just meant you weren't ready yet. Back when she told you that."

Kimber hopped up, obviously agitated. "What if I'm not good at sleepovers?" Her eyes widened. "What if I have an accident?"

An accident? Now things were getting tricky. Matt looked down the street, hoping for Minnie's white Grand Prix to appear out of nowhere. "Is that something that happens a lot?"

"No."

"Then you'll be okay." And with that bit of sage advice, little arms wrapped around him. He grunted. "Any girl who can squeeze me so tight should be able to handle a sleepover, no problem."

Kimber giggled. "When Minnie comes home, I'm going to call Nanci."

"You better call Minnie first and get permission. My door's open. Do you have her phone number?"

Kimber opened her hand to display seven numbers written almost neatly across her palm. "Yep."

"Go on in. You can use my phone and call her right now."

Just as she opened the screened door, he paused. "Hey, Kimber, when is the party?"

"Saturday night."

He couldn't help but smile. "I think you definitely need to give this party a try."

"Saturday night?" Minnie asked later that evening after he'd come over and they'd had another wonderful get-acquainted session on her couch.

"Yep." Matt could hardly keep the satisfaction from his voice. "Kimber will be gone for the evening, and Wanda will still be at the hospital—she's not scheduled to be released until Monday morning. You can come over and spend the night, Min."

"Okay," she said after a pause. Just like she'd just agreed to take his laundry to the cleaners.

"Am I rushing you? Do you want to wait until your parents are free? It's fine if you want to wait."

Her cheeks swam with color. "Not at all. Saturday night sounds fine."

"Good. Want to go out to eat first? We could go somewhere fancy."

"Would you mind if we ate at your place?"

"Not at all. I'll grill some fish."

"Okay."

Still a shadow hung around her eyes. Was there another secret she hadn't told him? "Hey, Min? You okay?"

"I am. Yes. I just…I just don't want you to be disappointed."

He gestured to the armrest of the couch, where minutes before they'd been half undressed. Where he'd pretty much shown her that he thought she was incredible. "You know I won't be."

Chapter Twenty-Four

On Saturday night, after depositing a very excited little girl at Nanci's house, Minnie went home, slipped on a brand-new lilac halter sundress and walked over to Matt's.

She wasn't sure what to expect. Candles? Romantic music? Matt half naked, eager to pull her into his bed?

Nope, he was dressed in a pale blue T-shirt and faded jeans and standing on a ladder. Changing a lightbulb.

Changing lightbulbs?

He looked down at her with a smile. "Hey, thanks for coming on in when I yelled. These always take longer to change than I figure they will."

Minnie put down her bag, an oversize tote with a nightgown, toothbrush and assorted hair accoutrements. Holding the ladder, she shook her head. "Matt Madigan, you constantly surprise me."

Holding the old lightbulb in his left hand, he stepped down two rungs. "What? Did you think you were going to come in here and get attacked?"

Now she felt silly. "I don't know."

After tossing the bulb into a nearby trash can, he hopped off the ladder and kissed her hello. "You look pretty."

"Thank you," she said, pleased. Matt would never have any idea how many outfits she'd tried on.

"I bought some tilapia at the market this morning, and some potatoes and salad, too. That sound okay?"

"Perfect."

"Good. I opened a bottle of wine. Would you pour two glasses? I'll take care of this stuff." Matt lifted up the ladder—and her tote—before she could say a word, and walked away.

Minnie had just put the bottle back in the fridge when Matt appeared again. "You want me to help make the salad?" she asked.

"Sure."

No, this was definitely not what Minnie had envisioned them doing. She worked beside him, cutting up vegetables and sipping wine. Slowly, her nervousness faded away, right about the time Alan Jackson was launching into his third song on the CD player.

They talked about Kimber, and Wanda's recovery and the mess in the attic while Matt cooked fish in the broiler. Matt poured more wine when it was time to eat.

They chatted some more, just like they were old friends. Which was what they'd always been, it seemed. Matt kept her entertained with stories about Jackie and Lane and their long-distance dating, and Minnie told him about two ladies who had come into her store that morning.

Then their food was gone. Minnie stood up. "I'll start on the dishes."

In a flash, Matt Madigan went from old friend to lover on the prowl. "Minnie, honey, how about we leave them for a while?"

Oh, there was that exaggerated drawl again. The one

that surfaced when he was aggravated or tired or—Minnie had come to find out—aroused.

Matt picked up her glass of wine and handed it to her. "Come out here, Min."

They walked out the back door into a twinkling wonderland. Sometime in the past twenty-four hours, Matt had put up what must have been a thousand twinkling white lights. Minnie stopped in her tracks. "This looks like something out of a movie."

He grinned. "I hope so. It took forever." He pointed to the pool. "So. We've eaten. Sipped some wine. Changed lightbulbs. Want to go skinny-dipping?"

Matt wasn't kidding. Nope, actually he looked kind of pleased with himself.

Minnie had assumed that the first time they would be naked together was in his bed. In the dark.

Not outside with the crickets.

"You skinny-dip a lot, Matt?"

"No." He pointed to the dense woods surrounding the backyard. Flashed a smile in the fading light. "But under the right circumstances, I've been known to enjoy it."

Minnie looked around again. Wanda's backyard had a high fence, lots of foliage and privacy. And, well, it was warm outside. She dipped a toe in the water. That was warm, too. Like bathwater.

Matt pulled off his shirt, revealing a chest that showed he certainly didn't just sit in an office all the time. Muscles played under his skin. A line of dark hair beat a path to the button of his jeans. "What do you say, Min? Wanna get naked?"

Minnie recalled how she'd felt just hours before when she'd packed her bag. She'd been a little nervous, but she was not with some stranger.

She was with Matt.

Matt, owner of sexy blue eyes and a gorgeous smile. The guy who could find humor in just about anything. Even hospital visits. Even old boyfriends and lost rodents. Even corporate growth.

Matt was caring and easy and full of surprises. And he wanted her.

"I'll get in the water, but I don't want you looking at me while I get undressed," she warned.

He scowled. "Shoot, Min."

"I'm not being unreasonable."

"You're not being any fun." He stepped closer. "How about I help with this tie at your neck?"

Minnie reached up and stilled his fingers. "Nope. Now, do what I say and turn around. I'll let you know when I'm all set."

"Minnie, I'm going to see you anyway."

"But not until I'm ready." Lifting her chin, she gave him her ultimatum. "This dress will not come off until I see your back."

"Fine." He turned. After two seconds, he called out, "You unknotted yet?"

"No."

"Minnie Clark, you're killing me."

She couldn't help it if she couldn't look away from his extremely well-proportioned back. At the indention along his spine. Her mouth went dry as she noticed that, unlike her, Matt didn't have a lick of inhibition about his body. With two deft movements, those jeans slid down past his hips. Down a pair of muscled thighs, landing in a pool at his feet.

Serviceable white briefs went next. As she'd always imagined, Matt Madigan had a pretty incredible backside.

"You naked yet, Min?"

"Not yet." Oh! She hoped he didn't notice that little hitch in her voice. "Don't turn around."

"I'm getting cold, standing here in my glory. You mind if I hop on in?"

"No. Well, not as long as you don't look."

She watched him neatly hop over the side with an easy splash. "Come on, Minnie. The water's warm."

It was now or never. Thinking what a shame it was that she'd bought a new dress and sexy underwear just for the great reveal, Minnie untied the halter, unfastened the row of buttons at her waist and stepped out of the dress. Off went the pretty pink lace panties. As the cool air brushed against her bare body, Minnie hurriedly went to the pool.

One, two, three steps in. She gasped as the water lapped against her thighs, then covered her belly button. Slowly she inched down until the pool surrounded her breasts.

Finally she was covered, but to Minnie's surprise, she felt no relief. The water was doing strange things to her insides. Unsettling her. Putting her on edge.

"I know you're in now," Matt said, and without waiting another moment, turned around. A warm glow of appreciation entered his eyes.

He approached slowly, his hands gently cutting through the water in easy strokes.

Minnie fought hard against covering herself. The dim lighting was doing a pretty good job. Anything he could see was shadowed by the water.

"You look pretty as a picture," he marveled, then swam a little closer.

Slow as molasses, he held out a hand. Minnie took it. And then, not so slowly, with one strong pull, he brought her up against him. The sudden shock of sliding against Matt's warm, bare body coaxed a thousand tremors through her. Oh, Lord. She wanted him something awful.

"Can you swim?" he murmured, his face so close to hers that she could feel his breath caress her cheek.

She rested her hands on his shoulders, felt the tips of her breasts brush against the wide expanse of his chest. "What?"

His hands rested on her back. Well, one did. The other was cupping her bottom. Every so often, their hips would bump against each other, reminding Minnie that there was nothing but a whole lot of patience separating them. "If I pull you deeper, you going to be okay?"

Matt was still talking about swimming. "Of course I can swim."

That was all he needed to know. With a fierce kick, he propelled them into the deep end, one of his hands holding her to him, the other navigating the top of the water.

Minnie gripped his biceps and gently kicked her legs, too. Then she adjusted herself as he pulled her close again and kissed her—full and openmouthed. For a split second, their bodies locked, flush against each other. Then, just as quickly, Matt released her and floated away.

She didn't know if she wanted him back or wanted to take a deep breath. Minnie settled for diving underwater and ruining her hairdo.

When she emerged, Matt was grinning. "Want to play Shark and Minnows?"

His look was so lascivious she couldn't resist playing along. "Let me guess, you're the big, bad shark."

There went that smile. "Do you want to be the shark? I'll let you catch me, Min."

"I'll be the minnow, thank you very much," Minnie said prissily, then darted away.

Matt hummed the *Jaws* theme and circled.

Before she knew it, Minnie was swimming for all her might, laughing when Matt would come in for a tag then swim away just as quickly. All of a sudden, she forgot to be worried about how she looked, or that they were both as naked as the days they were born.

Fact was, Matt Madigan made her happy, there was no doubt about it. And even if things between them ended awkwardly, or fairy-tale dreams never came true, Minnie knew she would always be grateful for this night.

She squealed as he grabbed her from behind, sinking his teeth into her neck. And then Minnie gasped for a whole different reason as Matt curved his arms around her front, seeking places that had nothing to do with childlike games.

"I've been dying to feel you, Min," he murmured, holding her gently, his hands over her breasts, his thumbs gently rubbing her distended nipples.

Minnie let her legs float, knowing she was safe in his arms. Hot kisses traipsed their way up her neck. Tickled her ear.

And one hand went far lower, cupping in between her legs, pushing her against his erection.

"Matt?"

"Hmm?"

"We ever going inside?"

Oh, those fingers of his certainly knew what to do. "You want to?" he murmured, his voice hoarse.

She was having a hard time talking. "Uh-huh."

"Okay, then."

To her surprise, they were in the shallow end. Without another word, Matt shifted his arms and picked her up. He carried her, sopping, dripping wet, right into the house. Minnie hung on and buried her face in his shoulder, loving the feel of Matt carrying her in his arms. Carrying her to his bed.

But they were awfully wet. "The carpet."

He chuckled. "Only you would worry about a carpet at a time like this."

She couldn't see his face, but she heard his smile. And because of that, she wasn't even embarrassed about her weight. About being stark naked with him.

About any of that.

He laid her on the bed, got out protection, then started kissing her before Minnie could even mention that a towel might be a good idea.

Instead, she held on tight and followed his lead, learning his body the way that he learned hers. Every so often, she'd look at him for direction, and he'd nod and shift and then caress her again.

And then, there it was. She was a virgin no more.

Holding his body above hers, he paused. "You okay?"

"I'm okay."

She caught a glimpse of that sexy smile right before the world tilted a little on its side. And Matt gasped her name.

Soon she did some gasping of her own.

And, oh, Lord have mercy. It had been so worth the wait.

Chapter Twenty-Five

"Minnie, I wanna come home."

Just minutes after their Big Event, Minnie's cell phone rang. Answering the phone while naked in Matt's arms was an altogether new experience, but the warm comfortable glow of their loving faded the moment Minnie heard Kimber's panicked voice.

"Can you come get me?"

Matt could hear Kimber's voice, too, loud and clear. He squeezed Minnie's shoulder in support.

"You want to tell me what's wrong?" Minnie asked, hoping for Kimber's sake that what the girl was feeling was just a simple case of the nerves. If she left in the middle of the party, the other girls might never let her forget it. "Maybe we can talk about it. I bet Nanci wants you to stay."

"No. I just want to go. Please, Aunt Minnie?"

Well, that title set off the alarm systems. Kimber never called her that anymore. "Okay, listen—"

"Oh, here's Mrs. Velasquez."

After a static shuffle, Nanci's mom came on. "Minnie?"

"Yes. Hi, Tracy."

"Listen, I think you'd better come on and get her. Kimber's been crying and looks a little shell-shocked."

Minnie struggled not to sound as distressed as she felt. "Anything happen?"

"I honestly don't know. All the girls were watching Disney movies and eating popcorn when Kimber started crying." A touch of exasperation entered her voice. "I tried to talk with her. Nanci did, too, but that didn't do a lot of good. She's pretty inconsolable."

Minnie didn't bother trying to explain away Kimber's behavior. Everyone around knew about Paige and Jeremy. No matter how hard Minnie tried to make everything good, the situation wasn't normal. "I'll be there in twenty minutes."

After she clicked off, she turned to Matt. "I guess I've got to go."

"I know you do. Poor little thing."

Minnie could have kissed him for saying that. "And poor us." She did give in to temptation and lean against him for a long minute. "I wasn't ready to leave."

"I'm not ready to say goodbye for the night." Pushing a strand of hair away from her face, he murmured, "Would you like some company?"

She would love it. But something told her that Kimber was going to need all her attention. "I don't think that would go over very well." With great regret, she pushed out of his arms. "I'm sorry."

Matt sat up, watching her with a concerned expression. When Minnie stretched and winced—her body had just used all kinds of new muscles—he frowned. "This isn't how I hoped the night would end."

"Me, neither."

Without a bit of unease, he watched her get

dressed. "So, Minnie, honey, are you going to be okay?"

Minnie wasn't sure if he was concerned about her body or the upcoming meeting with Kimber. She answered for both. "I think so." Quickly she buttoned her dress, glad Matt had brought their clothes in soon after they'd made love. "I'd better go."

Matt slipped on his jeans and walked her to the front door. But before she could say anything awkward, he reached for her wrist. "Hey," he murmured, pulling her close and smiling gently. "Tonight was wonderful."

Back came that blush. "I don't know—"

"It was unforgettable. Perfect. *You* were perfect. I promise."

Well. Minnie hadn't realized she needed to hear those words, but looking into his eyes and seeing his earnestness in the complete honesty written in his face, she felt like one of Kimber's princesses. Reaching up, she kissed him, holding his face in her palms, doing her best to tell him just how incredible she thought he was.

Just how special the night had been.

Matt responded like he'd been lit on fire. His mouth opened, and he kissed her deeply, bringing back memories of being so close to him that it seemed nothing could ever go wrong in her world.

Nothing else mattered.

She broke away. "I've got to go."

"Call me later?"

She nodded just as her cell phone started ringing again.

KIMBER WAS HAVING an honest-to-God breakdown in Minnie's car.

From the moment Minnie had appeared at the Velasquez's front door, the little girl had launched herself at Minnie and begun crying hysterically.

From behind Tracy, four concerned little faces peered out. Minnie tried to remember her manners and smile at the girls, all while picking up Kimber's sleeping bag, pillow and duffel bag, and shuffling her away. "Thanks for calling me. I'm sorry."

"Don't worry. She's had a hard time."

"I know," Minnie said, worry and regret filtering through her. Had she actually thought things were going to be okay, so quickly?

The counselor had said it could take over a year for Kimber to feel comfortable. At least.

Why had Minnie encouraged the sleepover, anyway? Had she really been that anxious to be with Matt? The answer came fast and furious. Yes, she had.

After putting the sleepover things in the trunk, Minnie walked Kimber to the backseat.

And then the tears began again. Minnie let her cry, thinking Kimber needed to blow off steam, but when it seemed her little niece was having trouble catching her breath, Minnie pulled over.

Then, there they sat, at ten at night in the parking area of Bluebonnet Park, Minnie doing her best to help Kimber but believing she wasn't doing very good at all.

"Honey, what happened?"

"I got scared."

"Of what?" Minnie racked her brain. "Were the other girls mean to you? Did you not like Mr. and Mrs. Velasquez?"

Kimber buried her head in her hands. "I liked them fine."

"Then what happened?"

"I...uh...I m-m...missed home. And then I forgot where home was."

"What do you mean?"

Through her hands, Kimber mumbled, "Home was in Arizona."

With a touch of surprise, Minnie finally understood what Kimber was talking about. "With your mom and dad."

After a moment, Kimber hiccupped. "I've tried to not miss 'em, but I do."

Oh, the words broke her heart. "You don't have to try not to miss them. You can miss your mom and dad all you want. I miss them, too." And though what she was saying brought forth more feelings of inadequacy, Minnie added, "Honey, I know you miss how things used to be. That's okay."

"Mommy used to play Barbies with me."

"I didn't know that." For the life of her, Minnie couldn't recall any Barbie dolls in Kimber's room. Treading carefully, she said, "I bet your mommy loved playing dolls with you. I used to tease her and say she was so pretty, she looked like a Barbie."

"She said I did, too."

"Where are all the dolls?"

Shamefaced, Kimber said, "I threw them away after Mommy and Daddy were put in the ground."

Minnie was stunned. "Why, sweetie?"

"I...I didn't want the dolls if I couldn't have Mommy."

Now Minnie was crying, too. How could she have lived with Kimber all this time and still be oblivious about so many of the girl's wants and fears? Only now was she finding out about Barbies and how hard Kimber had been trying to pretend that she was okay.

Minnie had thought she could do her best by Paige. But maybe that best was far, far from good enough. "Oh, sweetie. What are we going to do?" What was she going to do?

After a few more sniffles, Kimber answered, "Go back to your place?"

Not *their* place. *Not home.* Not yet.

Over the lump in her throat, Minnie nodded. "Sure." Slowly she edged out of the parking lot, taking care to watch for deer, and taking care to measure her words. "I bet you're tired."

"Uh-huh. And I miss George." After a few moments, Kimber spoke up again. "Are you mad?"

"What would I be mad about?"

"Because I miss how everything used to be?"

"Not at all. I miss your mommy, too. And your daddy. We can't help those feelings."

In the dark, Kimber sniffed. The sound made Minnie say more than she'd intended. "About the only thing I don't miss is my old life. I like having you with me, Kimber. I love your hugs and your pretty smiles. I love taking care of you. I missed you when you were in Arizona."

As Minnie turned onto their street, Kimber whispered, "I haven't been very nice all the time."

They'd come too far for Minnie to sugarcoat things. "That's okay."

"Why?"

"Sometimes you don't have to be nice. Sometimes you just have to be yourself. Being yourself and being happy with who you are is always the best way to go," Minnie said as they parked. The moment she said the words, Minnie felt her cheeks heat up. If ever anyone needed to take that advice, it was her!

After carefully unbuckling herself, Kimber scooted out of her booster seat and scrambled from the car. But then, to Minnie's surprise, she launched herself at Minnie. "I'm glad you came to get me."

"I'm glad, too," Minnie whispered. "Very glad."

Chapter Twenty-Six

Sunday morning dawned cloudy with a steady drizzle. Though she would've liked nothing better than to stay in bed, Minnie got up and dressed at Kimber's bidding, and took her to Sunday school.

To everyone's relief, after months of disquiet, Kimber had settled into the Noah's Ark themed room and had become a happy, enthusiastic participant.

While sitting in church, Minnie tried to focus on the sermon but it was useless. Her mind kept drifting back to Matt, their night together, and Kimber and her revelations. Each episode had been life changing and bittersweet.

She didn't know where things were going with Kimber. Chances were very good that they had a long, bumpy road ahead of them. But if Kimber finally trusted her and was settling in, maybe that's all that mattered. And then there was Matt. Were they now a couple? They'd never said much about the future.

After a quick lunch of fast food, they returned home to run smack into yet another crisis.

"George is gone!" Kimber said after running to her room to give a carrot to the guinea pig. "There's a big hole in the side of his cage!"

Minnie groaned. Couldn't she ever go just a few hours without something going wrong? Dutifully, she and Kimber went on a George hunt.

It wasn't too hard to find him, because he made such a racket. But what was surprising was what they found him doing. Nesting. Actually, George was lying somewhat morosely in the middle of a pile of towels and a batch of newspaper that he'd neatly shredded. He didn't show the slightest bit of interest in the carrot that Kimber was waving in front of his nose, either.

Minnie thought the little rodent was pudgier, too. That's when she had a pretty darn good idea of what was going on.

"George might be a girl, sweetie. I think she's fixing to have babies."

Brown eyes wide, Kimber knelt down and peered more closely at George's stomach. "Really?"

"Yep. We'll take her into the vet on Monday, but I think you're going to need another name for George. A girl name."

"Princess?"

"If you want, but George doesn't look very princessy to me." Minnie thought the guinea pig looked decidedly cranky and lethargic.

After patting the guinea pig gently on its head, Kimber stood up and clapped. "How about Georgia?"

Minnie couldn't help but chuckle. "That name sounds like a winner."

"Can we keep a baby?"

Minnie had an idea they definitely would. She just hoped she wouldn't get talked into keeping all the babies. "Let's cross that bridge when we get to it. In the meantime, we'd better fix Georgia's cage. Go get the big roll of silver tape, would you?"

ON MONDAY EVENING, Minnie arrived home from work and the babysitter's house to find Matt pacing outside on his front porch. The moment she waved hello, he trotted over.

Weariness was chased away by his gorgeous smile and an extremely warm kiss. "Hi," he murmured. "I missed you."

They'd talked on the phone a lot on Sunday evening but had agreed to spend the day apart. Matt had work and the house to prepare for Wanda's homecoming, and Minnie had been busy with Kimber and Georgia.

"I missed you, too," she said.

"Do you have a minute to talk?"

She looked over her shoulder. Kimber was already inside, sitting next to the guinea pig and reading out loud a new book from school. Early this morning, the vet had confirmed that George was definitely a "she" and definitely about to deliver. "I think I have quite a few minutes."

Minnie sat down on the top step and looked at Matt curiously as he moved to her side.

"Minnie, when Mrs. Wy comes home, I'm going to encourage her to stay here. Not just for a few months, like she's thinking, but for the next couple of years."

It wasn't the idea of Wanda returning to her home but of Matt leaving it that scared Minnie silly. "What about you?"

"I'm going to live there, too. I have to, Min." He paused for a moment, staring at his clasped hands draped over his knees. "She's going to need a lot of care. Someone to help get her things. Make sure she takes her medicine. Eats the right food. I owe her a lot, and I love her. She needs someone who cares about her close by."

"That's you."

"So…you understand?"

"Of course I do." How could she not? Matt was finally stepping forward and making attachments in Crescent View. Just as he'd always dreamed of doing.

But even as she celebrated Matt's decision, Minnie couldn't help but feel the weight of her own sinking emotions. With Wanda back home, there would be no more skinny-dipping sessions in his backyard. Well, not anytime soon.

Matt exhaled. "So how's Kimber? Is she still doing okay?"

"I think so." Glancing through the front window at the little girl, Minnie added, "But still, Saturday night made me realize that we've got a long way to go before either of us is ready to move on from Paige and Jeremy's deaths."

"All you can do is take things one step at a time. I think you might be doing better than you realize."

"Maybe." Minnie shrugged. "I sure hope so. Kimber and I talked a lot about Paige and Jeremy yesterday. A lot about her house in Arizona, and about all the things she used to do. Instead of trying so hard not to remind her of things that make her sad, we're going to put together a scrap book of old pictures, so her memories will be preserved." Just thinking about Kimber's wide-eyed expression when Minnie had mentioned the idea made her feel horrible. "I should've already done that, Matt."

"You've been doing the best you can. That's all you can ask of yourself."

"I suppose." Looking across the street at Matt's house and his truck in the parking lot, Minnie continued. "She had a good day at school—Nanci doesn't seem too mad. So, I guess we're going to be okay."

"And…George?"

"*Georgia* is fat and expecting." She rolled her eyes with a chuckle. "Oh, Matt. Only I would buy my daughter a pregnant guinea pig." Just as the words were out of her mouth, Minnie clasped a hand over her lips. "I didn't mean to say that. I know she's not my daughter. I meant—"

He stopped her words by gently removing her hand and bringing it to his lips instead. "You meant that you love her like a daughter."

"I do. She's as much my own now as if I'd given birth to her."

"I know that kind of feeling. I love Mrs. Wy like she was my mom for a lifetime." His eyes widened in surprise. "I don't think I've ever admitted that aloud before."

"That's a good sign, Matt."

Linking his fingers through hers, Matt said, "I guess we've both finally made some strong bonds, huh?"

He was right. They'd both been hoping for love and family…and each had found it in the most unexpected ways.

And…yet, she'd also found love with Matt. As he pressed his lips to her knuckles one more time, Minnie felt real fear.

She didn't want to go back to just being friends. She didn't even want to wait to be in his arms again. But how could they accept their other responsibilities if they didn't give them undivided attention?

And both Kimber and Wanda needed a lot of support and encouragement right now.

Their fingers still linked together, Matt murmured,

"About us…Minnie, I sure didn't mean to skinny-dip, love on you, and then move on."

Oh, the things he said! "You didn't."

He looked uncomfortable, like he was about to say he didn't like her mother. "The thing of it is, Minnie—"

She finished for him. "It's that we've got a lot of uncertainties right now. A lot of people who need our time and attention. Kimber is in a delicate place."

"So is Mrs. Wy. She almost died."

"And Kimber's the first person to ever really need me. I can't discount that."

"I'm in the same boat. Wanda needs someone looking out for her. She's going to need someone making sure that she doesn't go back to her old ways and start scarfing down lasagna like it's going out of style. That person needs to be me."

Minnie hated to bring their last obstacle up, but couldn't help herself. After all, their jobs were always there, looming in the background. "And, well, you've got Store 35 to get built."

He nodded. "I know I do. That takes up a lot of time." Blue eyes sparkled. "And you've got Carried Away and your SOS campaign."

"It's working. People are liking my section of local arts and crafts, too."

He winked. "Even SavNGo can't compete with that."

The excuses just kept coming. "And the holidays are just around the corner. It's going to be busy."

"Plans are already on the table for Store 36 in Abilene. I'm going to have to go out and get things organized there."

"So, it's real clear that now isn't the right time to start anything serious," Minnie finished softly, trying to keep the disappointment out of her tone. Though, truly, she already was serious about Matt. Had been for some time. Oh, she'd waited so long for him to be serious, too.

"I know you're right." The look in his eyes was full of relief. But also…regret? "I still care for you. I still want to see more of you."

It was as if Matt had read her mind. "We just need to step back for a bit and wait," she murmured. "I can do that."

Now that everything was settled, Matt grabbed her other hand, as if he wasn't anxious to release her even though their relationship was going nowhere. "I'm still glad about Saturday night," he murmured.

"Me, too." Since she had nothing to lose, Minnie spoke from the heart. "It was wonderful, Matt. Everything about it was perfect."

"I wish we had another night planned soon."

"I don't know if my heart could take it," she teased.

Pure pleasure filled his gaze. "It could. It would have been great."

It was only natural to lean into his arms and trade a kiss. He complied, touching her lips gently with his before stepping away. "Well, I'm going to go to the hospital."

Minnie peeked over her shoulder. "And I've got to read with Kimber and check on Georgia. We're on baby watch, you know."

"Call you later?"

"I'll do you one better. I'll bring y'all over a casserole when you get Wanda settled. Low fat."

Humor, as always, played in his expression. "I'll look forward to it."

As she watched Matt cross the street and start up his truck, Minnie tried to tell herself that everything was going to be okay. But it sure didn't feel that way.

She felt she was losing him.

Slowly, Matt's truck reversed. Backed down the driveway. She held up a hand to wave. Just in case he looked over her way.

"Minnie, come quick!"

She turned to see Kimber hopping up and down in the doorway. "What's wrong?"

"Georgia's squeaking somethin' awful!"

Standing up, she said, "Uh-oh. I'll be right there."

"Hurry!"

Minnie looked down the street before stepping inside. Maybe he was still there? Waiting to catch her eye one more time?

But Matt Madigan was gone. And though she'd said she didn't mind putting things off for a while, that waiting another couple of months or a year wouldn't be too difficult at all, Minnie knew she'd lied. Already she missed him.

Wanda Wyzecki could try the patience of a saint. As soon as he walked her into the house from the hospital, she started looking around with an eagle eye. "I didn't need to keep all those books and movies," she said, pointing to her chair and the shelf chock-full of her favorite romances and movies.

"Of course you needed to keep them. You're going to sit here and relax, right?"

"But you were supposed to make this your home."

"We're living together, remember?"

She peeked into the dining room. "Okay. I see a painting of yours, and your daddy's globe in the corner. But otherwise, things look the same."

"I don't have a dining room set." He shook his head.

Had Wanda really thought he was going to move out all her things while she'd been sitting in that hospital room? "Would you like to lie down for a bit?"

She had the nerve to glare at him when they walked into her old room. "Matthew, I don't see why I still have the master bedroom. You should have taken it over."

"I don't want your room, Wanda. I like mine just fine. Plus you don't need to be going up and down the stairs."

An hour later, Minnie and Kimber came and delivered a casserole. Though they only stayed long enough to hug Wanda, Matt felt a jolt of awareness simply from having Minnie in the same room.

As soon as they left, Wanda looked him over. "Something's different between you and Minnie."

"We're not arguing."

She eyed him a little more closely. "Nope, that's not it. There was something different about the way Minnie looked at you." Eyes widening, she gasped. "And Matthew, I saw you touch her."

Good grief! "What are you talking about, Wanda?"

"Oh, I saw you reach for her hand when those girls walked to the door. I saw you lean close to her when she put that diet casserole on the counter." Looking mighty pleased with herself, she nodded. "I know what I saw."

He couldn't deny it. Matt knew if he and Minnie had been alone, he'd have taken her back to his bed.

But no one else needed to know about that. "There's nothing wrong with touching Minnie."

She chuckled. "No, not a thing." She looked especially pleased as they walked into the living room. "So, I know y'all went to the movies. When are you taking her out again?"

Matt struggled to play it cool. "I don't know. We're both pretty busy right now."

"You can't work all the time, Matthew."

"It's not just work. Kimber's still struggling, and well…now's just not the right time."

"That doesn't make sense."

"I don't want to talk about it, okay?" He pointed to the kitchen. "You hungry yet?"

"No." She shooed him away. "You go do whatever you need to do, Matthew. Play with that BlackBerry or whatever. I'm going to sit here for a while and relax."

Matt knew better than to cross that tone. "Oh. Well, okay."

But as he walked upstairs to his room, Matt suspected Wanda wasn't quite as relaxed as she pretended to be.

Chapter Twenty-Seven

They settled into an awkward routine over the next month and a half. Matt worked and supervised construction, interviewed store managers, talked to vendors and did his best with the thousand other details involved in opening a new store. For two days every other week, he'd go to Philadelphia.

Minnie continued her SOS campaign and held an arts-and-crafts show the first weekend in October. It was a huge success. People came in to buy crafts and exited the store with all kinds of other cute things from Carried Away's shelves, including her new slightly expensive stationery. Already people were asking for Minnie to hold another fair closer to Christmas.

Jackie came out again to see Lane. Two weeks later, he flew up to Philadelphia to see Jackie and the big city. Matt had to spend the next few days after that hearing about how much Lane liked Jackie and hated the snow and sleet in Philly.

As the weather turned cooler, Minnie bought pumpkins and cornstalks and decorated the house and got ready for Halloween both at home and at Carried Away. She had a good meeting with the school counselor.

Kimber was crying less and reading more. She and Nanci were now best friends.

Georgia had three babies without much fanfare. Nanci was earmarked for one, Mrs. Strickland another and, as she expected, Minnie was destined to be a two guinea pig owner.

After a couple weeks of taking it easy, Wanda got up and about. She became a huge fan of grilled fish and salad and corn salsa. She took over cooking meals for her and Matt. Every so often, Minnie and Kimber joined them, too.

Wanda and Matt jokingly told Minnie how they'd gotten used to living with each other. They watched baseball together, but a lot of times kept to their own schedules, merely writing notes to each other on a blackboard Wanda installed in the kitchen.

Matt splurged on a cleaning lady to come in once a week so Wanda wouldn't be tempted to start scrubbing his shower. In return, Wanda did their laundry.

Sometimes Wanda came over and watched Kimber while Matt and Minnie went to the movies. But things never got too steamy or serious during those dates— Matt and Minnie knew they couldn't afford for things to get that way.

Yes, things were fine. *Fine.*

As the days became cooler and night descended on them earlier and earlier, Wanda and Kimber became close. Wanda started asking if Minnie would let Kimber ride the bus home and stay with her in the afternoons instead of at day care.

Minnie was so swamped with working and the holiday craziness, she accepted immediately. It soon became a regular thing to see Kimber out walking with Wanda.

And when Matt and Minnie did spend time together, well, they were cordial and good. Not heated and romantic.

Not like her dreams. Not like in that pool.

Cora Jean and Zenia and everyone else kept shopping at Carried Away and even had the audacity to ask Minnie why she'd ever been worried about keeping her customers.

Time was moving forward at a breakneck speed. Or slow as molasses. Depending who you talked to.

In fact, the only thing that seemed to bring a smile to Minnie's face was the prospect of Halloween and the cooler weather.

That, and the sweet, secretive smile Wanda and Kimber both wore. In fact, Minnie would've sworn they were plotting something if there'd been anything to plot.

A week before Halloween, when Minnie walked over to get Kimber after work, she seemed to interrupt a big meeting. "What are you doing here so soon?" Wanda asked, abruptly closing a notebook filled with scribbles.

Minnie couldn't help but feel unwanted. "Things were going well at Carried Away, so I decided to leave early. If, uh, that's okay."

Kimber sighed. "It sure would be nice if we all lived together. Then you wouldn't have to always hurry around."

"I like hurrying to see you, sweetheart."

Kimber beamed. "I like you, too. But still…" Eyes wide, she said, "Don't you wish Matt lived with us?"

"You silly. We'd have to be married to do that."

"You *could* get married, couldn't you?" Kimber twirled her newest skirt around. "Matt said he likes you a lot. Do you like Matt, too?"

"Of course I do." Minnie looked to Wanda for help,

but to her surprise, the older lady wasn't laughing. Instead, she wore that secretive smile.

"Then you could get married?"

"That's not how it works," Minnie said slowly. "People need to love each other. And, well, Matt hasn't asked me."

"Do you love him?"

"I…well…" Minnie knew she did. Shoot, she'd always loved him. And though Matt had never come right out and said it, she knew he cared for her deeply, too. No man would go to so much trouble for her first time otherwise.

Kimber had stopped spinning and was standing still as a statue. "Do you, Minnie?"

"That's enough, Kimber," Wanda said. "Go get your book bag so you and Minnie can go on home."

"If I lived here, I'd already be home."

Minnie pointed toward Wanda's utility room where a new, Kimber-size hook had just been installed for her book bag. "Go."

When they were alone, Minnie rolled her eyes. "Where do you think that all came from?"

Wanda shrugged. "No telling. Kids say the darnedest things."

Minnie nodded in agreement, but as she held Kimber's hand and walked across the street, she got the feeling that maybe everything wasn't as coincidental as she'd first thought. Maybe not by a long shot.

MINNIE HAD JUST BOUGHT some material to make Kimber's costume for trick-or-treating when Wanda threw a wrench in that plan, a mere two days before the thirty-first.

"Minnie, Kimber and I've been talking and we decided we're going trick-or-treating together. That is, if you don't mind."

Seeing how excited they both looked at the prospect, Minnie didn't mind at all. But she wasn't sure Wanda was up to the task. "Wanda, it will be a lot of walking. Are you sure you'll be up for that?"

"I'm feeling fine. I've been walking every day on my treadmill, you know."

"I'm going to take care of Mrs. Wy," Kimber said importantly. "She's going to tell me if she gets too tired. Plus, we're going to get walkie-talkies."

They were beaming like they'd been planning the next big adventure. There was no way Minnie was going to interfere. Kimber needed as many people in her life as possible to count on and, without a doubt, there was no one better than Wanda Wyzecki. "Okay. I guess I'll stay home and give out candy." Minnie pointed to the pile of fabric. "Now, I was thinking about your costume, and—"

Kimber and Wanda shared another secret smile. "We've already got our costumes figured out, too," Wanda said. "We're going to be the Little Red Riding Hood and the Big Bad Wolf."

Tapping her chest, Kimber proclaimed, "I'm gonna be Little Red Riding Hood."

Minnie chuckled. "Wanda, I've never pictured you as a wolf."

"I'm full of surprises," Wanda replied cryptically.

Pretty much everything seemed to be, Minnie thought.

THE NEXT EVENING, when Minnie's water heater went on the fritz, Matt came over. "I heard you've been needing a handyman."

Minnie chuckled. "You sound almost naughty, talking like that."

Before she knew it, Matt reached for her and kissed her quick. "I can't help it. I'm feeling naughty."

Well, there she went. Her body got all hot and bothered in seconds. "You shouldn't talk like that. Kimber's upstairs."

"She won't know what I mean," he murmured before stealing another kiss. And another.

Dislodging herself from Matt's embrace, Minnie said, "She will if we don't stop kissing."

"I don't want to stop."

"We're taking a break," she reminded him.

He scowled. "I'm sick of our break."

She was, too. "Maybe we can speed things up after Christmas? It will be a year since Kimber moved in, then."

"That sounds good. Wanda will be a lot better come January." Grabbing his toolbox, Matt went into the laundry room closet and inspected things. "In the meantime, hand me a wrench."

Minnie peered in over his shoulder as she did what he asked. "Thanks for coming out. I didn't know who else to call."

"I'm glad you did."

"But you had to leave work early. I thought maybe one of the guys at the site could come out."

"No self-respecting Texan is going to admit to his crew that he can't fix a water heater." With a grunt, Matt tightened some bolts with the wrench before backing out of the tight space.

They walked to the front entryway. Unable to resist touching him, Minnie brushed off a piece of lint from his navy T-shirt. "I guess you heard about Wanda and Kimber trick-or-treating together?"

"Yep. You and I will be all alone in our houses, passing out Snickers bars." He leaned forward. "I'll send you signals from across the way."

"I'll look forward to it."

She'd just raised her lips to his, not caring who saw them kissing, when Kimber appeared. "Matt, want to see Georgia's babies?"

He turned her way. "Are they cuter? They weren't much to look at when they were born."

"They're super-cute now!" Kimber grabbed his hand. "Come on, Matt."

With a wink Minnie's way Matt let himself be dragged down the hall and out of sight.

Frustration roared inside her. For the first time in her life, Minnie hoped the holidays would pass in a rush.

THE DOORBELL hadn't rung in twenty minutes. It was getting late. Where was Kimber?

Minnie peered out across the street, but didn't see any ghostly trick-or-treaters who looked like a wolf and Little Red Riding Hood.

Nope, just a few scraggly groups of kids and the fading glow of jack-o'-lanterns.

Now Minnie was getting worried. Where could they be? Maybe Wanda had had a heart problem and she and Kimber were stuck somewhere on a corner, waiting for help?

Now she was just scaring up problems. If two people were in trouble, anyone in the neighborhood would be coming to their rescue—and rushing to tell Minnie.

Minnie closed the door and went back to her spot by the couch and the big bowl of candy. As usual, she'd bought too much. If she wasn't careful, she was going to gain ten pounds from her addiction to Twix bars.

Giving in to the inevitable, she grabbed one and tore off the wrapper.

The doorbell rang just after she'd taken two bites. Before she could swallow all the chocolate and caramel, the doorbell chimed again.

"Hold on, I'm hurrying." Quickly she grabbed the bowl of candy and pulled open the door.

And stood there in surprise. Kimber and Wanda—and Matt—were on her front porch.

"Hi."

"Trick or treat!" Wanda said, with only her eyes, nose, and mouth peeking out from a furry wolf mask.

Dutifully, Minnie got her bowl. "Okay. Take as much—"

"We don't want treats!" Kimber exclaimed. "We got a trick."

Minnie looked at Matt, who seemed as puzzled as she was. "I got the same treatment, Min." With a bemused look at Kimber, he added, "I got 'tricked,' too."

Wanda took charge. "We need to have an important discussion," she said, pulling off her wolf mask and leading the way into the living room.

Minnie followed. Matt closed the door behind them and finished up the procession. Curious, she sat down across from the three of them. "What's going on?"

"We decided, Kimber and I, that it's time we all came to some decisions. It's time you and Matt resolved some things."

"What are y'all talking about?" Minnie glanced toward Matt.

He merely shrugged. "I'm as clueless as you are, Min."

Kimber hopped up and put one finger to her cherry-red painted lips. "Shh!"

Wanda smiled. "Thank you. Now it's time to get down to business. Minnie and Matt, for the last few months you two have been driving us crazy."

Matt propped one boot-covered foot over his knee. "This is what you needed to share?"

"No," said Kimber. "But I've seen you kissing. A lot."

Minnie felt herself blushing. "I'm sorry you saw us."

"Don't you like kissing Matt?"

"Yes, I like kissing Matt a lot."

Matt held up a hand. "Wanda, this doesn't seem like a very appropriate conversation."

Wanda slipped an arm around Kimber. "Don't get all riled up. What I'm saying is that I think you two ought to just settle down and finally realize that you are meant to be together. You two have something special. Is it love?"

Minnie knew it was. "Yes?"

Wanda narrowed her eyes. "Are you sure?"

Seeing the emotion in Matt's eyes, Minnie answered again, this time with her heart leading the way. "Yes. I'm sure." Shoot, she'd always been sure.

With a look that she'd most likely perfected in 1950, Wanda directed a glare Matt's way. "Matthew, what do you have to say?"

"I love Minnie, too." He leaned forward. "But you already knew that, right?"

She nodded. "I knew."

Right before Matt could say anything else, Wanda cleared her throat. "I knew it, too."

Blotches of red stained his cheeks. "Jeez, Wanda. Do we have to do this now? All together?"

"Yes." Wanda folded her arms over her very furry wolf chest. Amazingly, even dressed up, she could still cow Matt. When he still didn't say a word, she tapped a paw. "Matthew?"

He scowled. "Fine." Standing up, Matt walked over to Minnie. "I love you, Minnie. I've loved you for some time, I've just been trying to get the courage to say it. Words are hard for me." He took her hands, as if they were alone.

"I know they are. I love you, too." And just like always, Minnie's hands felt right in his. Perfect. Oh, she loved him so!

But Wanda had to go ahead and interrupt. Again. "Matthew. Minnie. Don't y'all think it's time you two stopped your pussyfooting around and took some vows?"

"Marriage vows!" Kimber interjected, jumping up and down in her red satin cape and shiny patent Mary Janes.

Matt leaned close. Brushed his lips against her cheek. "Minnie, honey, will you marry me? Will you finally be mine, for always and forever?"

"I will."

Wanda wiped her eyes. "That's a real nice proposal, Matthew."

He answered Wanda all while sharing a smile with Minnie. "Yes, ma'am."

Kimber cheered.

Right after Matt brushed his lips over hers, Minnie turned to their audience. "Now that I'm an engaged woman…do you two care to explain what's going on?"

Wanda wasted no time in replying. "It's easy. Little Red and I decided we want us all to be together. All four of us."

"In one house," Kimber said. "Just like we were a family."

No, it *would* be a family. A mixed-up, patchwork, imperfect one. Minnie's favorite kind. Still holding both of Matt's hands, she looked up at him. "What do you think? Do you want to give this a try?"

Blue eyes sparkled. "Very much. Let's not wait any longer. Let's get married and be together, all of us."

Stealing a glance at Kimber and Wanda, Minnie nodded. "We'll live happily ever after. All four of us. Finally."

ONCE UPON A TIME, Minnie Clark had loved Matt Madigan.

Then he'd gone away, and she'd been sure her day-dreams had only been childish fantasies.

And then, years later, Matt had returned. But he hadn't been perfect.

She hadn't been, either.

For a brief moment, she'd had Matt. But she had a whole lot of other things, too.

It had taken an elderly lady and a curly-headed girl to remind her that fairy tales could still come true—even if they weren't quite picture-perfect.

And just as Matt leaned down to kiss her once again, and as Kimber raced toward them for a hug, Minnie said the words that had been in her heart for quite some time.

"Matt, I'm glad you came back. I'm so glad you returned to Crescent View."

She was so glad he'd come back to her.

* * * * *

'I'VE FOUND HER.'

Max froze.

It was what he'd been waiting for since June, but now—now he was almost afraid to voice the question. His heart stalling, he leaned slowly back in his chair and scoured the investigator's face for clues. 'Where?' he asked, and his voice sounded rough and unused, like a rusty hinge.

'In Suffolk. She's living in a cottage.'

Living. His heart crashed back to life, and he sucked in a long, slow breath. All these months he'd feared—

'Is she well?'

'Yes, she's well.'

He had to force himself to ask the next question. 'Alone?'

The man paused. 'No. The cottage belongs to a man called John Blake. He's working away at the moment, but he comes and goes.'

God. He felt sick. So sick he hardly registered the next few words, but then gradually they sank in. 'She's got *what?*'

'Babies. Twin girls. They're eight months old.'

'Eight—?' he echoed under his breath. 'They must be his.'

He was thinking out loud, but the P.I. heard and corrected him.

'Apparently not. I gather they're hers. She's been there since mid-January last year, and they were born during the summer—June, the woman in the post office thought. She was more than helpful. I think there's been a certain amount of speculation about their relationship.'

He'd just bet there had. God, he was going to kill her. Or Blake. Maybe both of them.

'Of course, looking at the dates, she was presumably pregnant when she left you, so they could be yours, or she could have been having an affair with this Blake character before…'

He glared at the unfortunate P.I. 'Just stick to your job. I can do the math,' he snapped, swallowing the unpalatable possibility that she'd been unfaithful to him before she'd left. 'Where is she? I want the address.'

'It's all in here,' the man said, sliding a large envelope across the desk to him. 'With my invoice.'

'I'll get it seen to. Thank you.'

'If there's anything else you need, Mr Gallagher, any further information—'

'I'll be in touch.'

'The woman in the post office told me Blake was away at the moment, if that helps,' he added quietly, and opened the door.

Max stared down at the envelope, hardly daring to open it, but when the door clicked softly shut behind the P.I., he eased up the flap, tipped it and felt his breath jam in his throat as the photos spilled out over the desk.

Oh, lord, she looked gorgeous. Different, though. It

took him a moment to recognise her, because she'd grown her hair, and it was tied back in a ponytail, making her look younger and somehow freer. The blond highlights were gone, and it was back to its natural soft golden-brown, with a little curl in the end of the ponytail that he wanted to thread his fingers through and tug, just gently, to draw her back to him.

Crazy. She'd put on a little weight, but it suited her. She looked well and happy and beautiful, but oddly, considering how desperate he'd been for news of her for the past year—one year, three weeks and two days, to be exact—it wasn't only Julia who held his attention after the initial shock. It was the babies sitting side by side in a supermarket trolley. Two identical and absolutely beautiful little girls.

* * * * *

When Max Gallagher hires a P.I. to find his estranged wife, Julia, he discovers she's not alone— she has twin baby girls, and they might be his. Now workaholic Max has just two weeks to prove that he can be a wonderful husband and father to the family he wants to treasure.

Look for TWO LITTLE MIRACLES
by Caroline Anderson,
available February 2009 from Harlequin Romance®.

HARLEQUIN Romance®

This February the Harlequin® Romance series
will feature six Diamond Brides stories featuring
diamond proposals and gorgeous grooms.

Share your dream wedding proposal and you could WIN!

The most romantic entry will win a diamond
necklace and will inspire a proposal in one of
our upcoming Diamond Grooms books in 2010.

In 100 words or less, tell us the most romantic
way that you dream of being proposed to.

For more information, and to enter
the Diamond Brides Proposal contest, please visit
www.DiamondBridesProposal.com

Or mail your entry to us at:

IN THE U.S.: 3010 Walden Ave., P.O. Box 9069, Buffalo, NY 14269-9069
IN CANADA: 225 Duncan Mill Road, Don Mills, ON M3B 3K9

REQUEST YOUR FREE BOOKS!
2 FREE NOVELS PLUS 2
FREE GIFTS!

Love, Home & Happiness!

YES! Please send me 2 FREE Harlequin® American Romance® novels and my 2 FREE gifts (gifts are worth about $10). After receiving them, if I don't wish to receive any more books, I can return the shipping statement marked "cancel." If I don't cancel, I will receive 4 brand-new novels every month and be billed just $4.24 per book in the U.S. or $4.99 per book in Canada. That's a savings of close to 15% off the cover price! It's quite a bargain! Shipping and handling is just 25¢ per book, along with any applicable taxes.* I understand that accepting the 2 free books and gifts places me under no obligation to buy anything. I can always return a shipment and cancel at any time. Even if I never buy another book from Harlequin, the two free books and gifts are mine to keep forever.

154 HDN EEZK   354 HDN EEZV

Name _____ (PLEASE PRINT) _____

Address _____ Apt. # _____

City _____ State/Prov. _____ Zip/Postal Code _____

Signature (if under 18, a parent or guardian must sign)

Mail to the **Harlequin Reader Service:**
IN U.S.A.: P.O. Box 1867, Buffalo, NY 14240-1867
IN CANADA: P.O. Box 609, Fort Erie, Ontario L2A 5X3

Not valid to current subscribers of Harlequin® American Romance® books.

Want to try two free books from another line?
Call 1-800-873-8635 or visit www.morefreebooks.com.

* Terms and prices subject to change without notice. N.Y. residents add applicable sales tax. Canadian residents will be charged applicable provincial taxes and GST. Offer not valid in Quebec. This offer is limited to one order per household. All orders subject to approval. Credit or debit balances in a customer's account(s) may be offset by any other outstanding balance owed by or to the customer. Please allow 4 to 6 weeks for delivery. Offer available while quantities last.

Your Privacy: Harlequin is committed to protecting your privacy. Our Privacy Policy is available online at www.eHarlequin.com or upon request from the Reader Service. From time to time we make our lists of customers available to reputable third parties who may have a product or service of interest to you. If you would prefer we not share your name and address, please check here. ☐

HAR08R2

You're invited to join our Tell Harlequin Reader Panel!

By joining our new reader panel you will:

- Receive Harlequin® books—they are FREE and yours to keep with no obligation to purchase anything!
- Participate in fun online surveys
- Exchange opinions and ideas with women just like you
- Have a say in our new book ideas and help us publish the best in women's fiction

In addition, you will have a chance to win great prizes and receive special gifts! See Web site for details. Some conditions apply. Space is limited.

To join, visit us at
www.TellHarlequin.com.

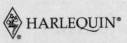

HARLEQUIN®

American ★ Romance®

COMING NEXT MONTH

#1245 ONCE A LAWMAN by Lisa Childs
Men Made in America
To protect and serve is the credo Chad Michalski has always lived by. But who's going to protect *him* from the vivacious blonde he just pulled over for speeding? Tessa Howard's recklessness has landed her in the Lakewood Citizens Police Academy, where the widowed cop can keep a close eye on her...and fight a losing battle against their growing attraction.

#1246 THE SECRET AGENT'S SURPRISES by Tina Leonard
The Morgan Men
Secret agent Pete Morgan has never considered himself a family man. Until he returns to Texas to collect his inheritance...and meets quadruplet babies in need of a home. To adopt the four tiny angels, Pete needs a wife. Prim, proper and wildly attractive Priscilla Perkins is the perfect candidate. Besides, it's just a temporary engagement. *Isn't it?*

#1247 ONCE UPON A VALENTINE'S by Holly Jacobs
American Dads
Single mom Carly Lewis thinks it's oh-so-ironic that she's organizing the local school's Valentine's Day dance! Cue the music *and* hunky Lieutenant Chuck Jefferson, the good-natured cop who wears his badge proudly on his chest and his heart on his sleeve. They've each been burned by love, so Cupid's working overtime this holiday to show these two how special they are together....

#1248 THE MAN SHE MARRIED by Ann DeFee
Maizie Walker is in a funk. After twenty years of marriage, all she wants is a little more attention from her husband, Clay. What's a girl to do? Make him jealous, of course! Maizie's convinced that flirting with another man will make Clay sit up and take notice. But when her plan backfires and Clay moves out, can Maizie ever get him back?

www.eHarlequin.com